純真年代

THE AGE OF INNOCENCE

Edith Wharton

改寫 _ Nora Nagy
譯者 _ 蔡裴驊

About Your Book

🎧 Listen to the story.

🗩 Talk about the story.

ⓟ Prepare for Cambridge English Exams: B1 Preliminary.

FACT FILE Read informative fact files which develop themes from the story.

LIFE SKILL Draw comparisons between the story and contemporary life.

e·ZONE ONLINE ACTIVITIES Go to Helbling e-zone to do activities.

For the Teacher

A state-of-the-art interactive learning environment with 1000s of free online self-correcting activities for your chosen readers.

Go to our Readers Resource site for information on using readers and downloadable Resource Sheets, photocopiable Worksheets and Answer Keys. Plus free sample tracks from the story.
helbling.com/english

For lots of great ideas on using Graded Readers, consult Reading Matters, the Teacher's Guide to using Helbling Readers.

Contents

About the Author

Edith Wharton was born Edith Newbold Jones in January 1862, into a wealthy New York family. Her family traveled a lot in Europe, and Edith spent six years of her childhood living in Italy, France and Germany.

She studied French and German, and when her family returned to New York in 1872, she was tutored[1] at home. Edith was fortunate to have access[2] to her father's library. She read and studied a lot, and her first collection of poems was printed privately in 1876.

At age 17, she was presented to society, which meant that she could go to parties and dances in Newport and New York. She criticized[3] the rituals[4] of this world in her novels. In 1885 she married Edward (Teddy) Wharton, who shared her love of travel.

She developed a passion[5] for design and gardening, and designed The Mount, the house where she lived for ten years. She continued to travel in Europe with her husband or friends, including the author Henry James. Edith also had a long love affair with the journalist[6] Morton Fullerton. She sold The Mount in 1912, then divorced her husband and moved to Paris.

When World War I broke out, she helped the war effort[7] by establishing workplaces for women, hostels[8] for refugees[9], and new hospitals. She also published articles about the war and received the French Legion of Honor for her work.

After the war she lived and wrote in a village in the south of France. She won the Pulitzer Prize[10] for *The Age of Innocence* in 1921, which made her the first woman to win the award.

She died on 11 August 1937, and she was buried in Versailles, next to her long-time friend Walter Berry.

---

1 tutor [ˈtjutɚ] (v.) 輔導
2 access [ˈæksɛs] (n.) 進入
3 criticize [ˈkrɪtɪˌsaɪz] (v.) 評論
4 ritual [ˈrɪtʃʊəl] (n.) 儀式
5 passion [ˈpæʃən] (n.) 熱情
6 journalist [ˈdʒɝnəlɪst] (n.) 新聞記者
7 war effort 戰爭時期的努力
8 hostel [ˈhɑstl] (n.) 旅舍（尤其指青年旅館）
9 refugee [ˌrɛfjʊˈdʒi] (n.) 難民
10 Pulitzer Prize 普立茲獎

ABOUT THE BOOK

Wharton wrote *The Age of Innocence* in France, just after World War I. She was an established writer at the time and had already published a number of novels and novellas[1]. The title refers to a period in American history which had come to an end with the war in 1914.

Indeed, in the book she looks back on her childhood and teenage years in the high society of New York in the 1870s, with its balls, dances and rigid[2] rules. The 1870s in America is also called the Gilded Age: a time when bankers and investors[3] became influential, and the city of New York began to grow rapidly. At that time, society was controlled by powerful families who had strong traditions and strict yet often unwritten rules.

1 novella [noˈvɛlə] (n.) 中篇小説
2 rigid [ˈrɪdʒɪd] (a.) 嚴格的
3 investor [ɪnˈvɛstɚ] (n.) 投資者
4 engagement [ɪnˈgedʒmənt] (n.) 訂婚
5 complication [ˌkɑmpləˈkeʃən] (n.) 混亂；複雜
6 threaten [ˈθrɛtn̩] (v.) 威脅
7 irony [ˈaɪrənɪ] (n.) 諷刺
8 intention [ɪnˈtɛnʃən] (n.) 意圖
9 pervading [pɚˈvedɪŋ] (a.) 遍及的
10 renowned [rɪˈnaʊnd] (a.) 有名的

The novel tells the story of the engagement[4] and marriage of May Welland and Newland Archer, and the arrival of Ellen Olenska, the bride's cousin from Europe. Ellen's presence leads to a series of complications[5] and threatens[6] the couple's marriage.

Wharton looks back on this age with irony[7] but without judging any of the characters' intentions[8] and actions. Apart from her criticism of the workings of upper-class society, there is a pervading[9] sense of sadness over the loss of innocence brought about by World War 1. Wharton's own life experiences are reflected in the novel from her early memories, to her unsuccessful marriage.

The novel won the Pulitzer Prize in 1921 and inspired several film adaptations, including the renowned[10] 1993 film directed by Martin Scorsese starring Daniel-Day Lewis, Winona Ryder and Michelle Pfeiffer.

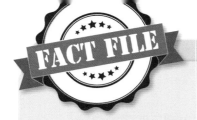

New York Society in the 1870s

New York society in the 1870s was a very organized system. It was structured like a pyramid[1] with the most influential and powerful families on the top, the fashionable elite[2] just under and the newcomers on the bottom.

The old families were apprehensive[3] of the new people as they had new values and rules and posed[4] a threat to the former's authority[5]. The new families often lived according to different rules or had become rich too quickly, like the Beauforts in the novel.

The 400

At that time an estimated 400 people belonged to the most fashionable circle of New York families. The name comes from the Astor family's ballroom, which was big enough for 400 guests. These families, for example the Astors, the Rockefellers and the Vanderbilts were also called New York High Society. They became powerful either because of their British, Dutch or French heritage[6] or thanks to their investment in growing businesses.

Their wealth was always on display[7]. There were chandeliers[8], silverware[9] and artworks shown at every social occasion such as weddings, dinners and balls. The women wore luxurious dresses with satin[10], velvet, feathers, and expensive jewelry.

1 pyramid [ˈpɪrəmɪd] (n.) 金字塔
2 elite [eˈlit] (n.) 菁英分子
3 apprehensive [ˌæprɪˈhɛnsɪv] (a.) 憂慮的
4 pose [poz] (v.) 造成
5 authority [əˈθɔrətɪ] (n.) 權威
6 heritage [ˈhɛrətɪdʒ] (n.) 遺產
7 display [dɪˈsple] (v.) (n.) 展出；顯示
8 chandelier [ˌʃændlˈɪr] (n.) 枝形吊燈
9 silverware [ˈsɪlvəˌwɛr] (n.) 銀製品
10 satin [ˈsætɪn] (n.) 緞

The codes[1]

In the novel, the customs and traditions of these families are described as "rituals" and the families as "tribes." If someone broke the rules of society, they were punished. These rules or codes controlled every aspect of people's lives from matters of social status through annual routines to everyday behavior. For example, divorce was

unacceptable; balls, opera nights and other social occasions were standard fixtures everyone was expected to attend and going out on Sunday was not fashionable.

The places

New York's elite could be seen in a number of socially acceptable places such as the opera house or private ballrooms and dinner parties. Balls and dinners were obviously more private events while the opera houses were more public. Having one of the eighteen opera boxes at the Academy of Music was an important status[2] symbol.

The most fashionable areas in the city were found between 3rd and 6th Avenues, and most upper-class families did not move north of Central Park. Old families lived on Washington Square and in its neighborhood. When they left the city, their destinations were typically Newport and Rhineback.

The rest of the society

There were artists and writers, who could not afford to live in the rich areas of the city. They lived in the bohemian[3] quarters[4] of the city. The poor working classes lived in badly constructed and overcrowded apartment buildings. Six or seven people often had to share a bedroom without windows or a bathroom.

1 code [kod] (n.) 規範
2 status [ˋstetəs] (n.) 地位；身分
3 bohemian [boˋhimɪən] (a.) 波西米亞風格的；放蕩不羈的
4 quarter [ˋkwɔrtɚ] (n.)（城市中的）區

THE GILDED AGE

The period between 1865 and 1898 in American history is often called the Gilded[1] Age. It was the time after the Civil War (1861–1865) when economic[2] and technological[3] development were at a height. It ended with the Spanish-American War.

The name comes from the book *The Gilded Age: A Tale of Today* written by Mark Twain and Charles Dudley Warner in 1873, which described the political corruption[4] and the social issues[5] of the time. The word "gilded" in the title refers to a thin layer of gold covering problems under the surface.

Economic power

This was a time of fast economic growth. Both wages[6] and the personal wealth of bankers and industrialists[7] were increasing quickly. The agricultural industry and coal mining were thriving[8], but the most successful industries[9] were the new oil, railway and steel corporations.

John D Rockefeller and John D Rockefeller Jr in 1915

Cornelius Vanderbilt and his wife Grace on Fifth Avenue, New York

Economic power was in the hands of a few wealthy men and their families, such as John D. Rockefeller, Andrew Carnegie, J. P. Morgan and Cornelius Vanderbilt. They were known as the "robber barons" because they had become rich and powerful by exploiting[10] the working classes and manipulating[11] the political scene.

In this period, Wall Street in New York was established as the center of the financial market .

The Robber Barons
What do you know about these families? What are they famous for today? Find out online.

1	gilded [ˈgɪldɪd] (a.) 鍍金的	7 industrialist [ɪnˈdʌstrɪəlɪst] (n.) 實業家
2	economic [ˌikəˈnɑmɪk] (a.) 經濟上的	8 thriving [ˈθraɪvɪŋ] (a.) 繁榮的
3	technological [ˌtɛknəˈlɑdʒɪkl̩] (a.) 技術的	9 industry [ˈɪndəstrɪ] (n.) 產業
4	corruption [kəˈrʌpʃən] (n.) 貪污；腐壞	10 exploit [ɪkˈsplɔɪt] (v.) 剝削
5	issue [ˈɪʃju] (n.) 議題；問題	11 manipulate [məˈnɪpjəˌlet] (v.) 操作
6	wage [wedʒ] (n.) 薪水	

Technology

This period is also called the Second Industrial Revolution[1]. The Gilded Age could not have happened without technological development and the introduction of mass production and transportation.

Steel[2] production became easier and faster and this led to the building of railroads. The Pacific Railroad (the First Transcontinental Railroad) opened in 1869. It took travelers only six days to get from New York in the East to San Francisco in the West. Most of the steel industry was around Chicago, which was also growing quickly.

Another important area of development was communication and electricity[3]. The American Telephone and Telegraph Company was founded in 1885. It still exists today as one of the biggest telephone companies, AT&T. Electricity brought important changes: streets and houses had electric power. With artificial lighting, people could work more but it also meant that they slept less.

There were electric streetcars in the major cities. It became easier to get to places and to talk to people, and business transactions[4] also became faster.

Refrigeration[5], especially for meat, was another important improvement, because it made it easier to transport meat from faraway places.

Immigrant workers

A lot of immigrant[6] workers arrived from Eastern Europe, Russia and Italy. They lived in small apartments and worked in the factories. During the Gilded Age about 11.7 million people arrived in the United States. These people contributed to the economic growth of the age. Most of them lived in extremely poor conditions and often worked up to twelve hours a day. They are often referred to as the people "who built America."

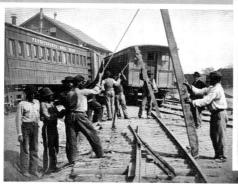

1   Industrial Revolution 工業革命
2   steel [stil] (n.) 鋼鐵
3   electricity [ˌilɛkˈtrɪsətɪ] (n.) 電力
4   transaction [trænˈzækʃən] (n.) 交易
5   refrigeration [rɪˌfrɪdʒəˈreʃən] (n.) 冷凍
6   immigrant [ˈɪməgrənt] (a.) 移民的

The Age of Innocence

Newland Archer

Monsieur Riviére

Mrs Archer

Countess Ellen Olenska

May Welland

Julius & Regina Beaufort

the van der Luydens

Mrs Mingott & Mrs Welland

BEFORE READING

1 Read the extract from the story and then answer the question.

When Newland Archer opened the door at the back of the box he shared with his friends, the opera had already begun. He was not worried about his late arrival. It was not "the thing" to arrive early at the opera, and what was or was not the thing was important to Newland Archer.

Does Newland Archer agree or disagree with the conventions of his friends?

2 Listen to Newland Archer's thoughts on his relationships then tick (✓) T (true) or F (false).

T **F** (a) Newland's future wife loved reading.
T **F** (b) Newland's future wife was innocent.
T **F** (c) The married woman was charming.
T **F** (d) The married woman was happy.

3 The words on the right are used in the story to describe Newland Archer's fiancée, and then wife, May. Look up the ones you don't know in a dictionary. Are these characteristics important to you in other people? Put them in order of importance (1-8).

☐ innocent
☐ conventional
☐ beautiful
☐ intelligent
☐ popular
☐ reasonable
☐ nice
☐ simple

2 4 Ellen Olenska is an important character in the story. Complete this description of her using the words below. Then listen and check.

> mysterious late drawing room
> voice simple

On the night of the dinner, Countess Olenska arrived
a _____ at the van der Luydens', but she
entered the b _____ without any hurry or
embarrassment. When she paused in the middle of the
room, Archer noticed her c _____ beauty
and d _____ behavior. She was quiet in her
movements and e _____, and not as stylish as
everyone had expected her to be.

5 Look at Exercises **3** and **4** again. How do you imagine May and Ellen? Share ideas with a friend.

Ellen

_____
_____
_____
_____

May

_____
_____
_____
_____

19

6 Match the places on the left with the definitions on the right.

_____ a club
_____ b ballroom
_____ c drawing room
_____ d opera house

1 a theater where operas are performed
2 the place where the members of an organization meet
3 a large room used for dancing
4 the main room in a house where guests are received

7 This story is about relationships in New York society in the 1870s. Look at the picture and then use the words in the box to complete the sentences from the story.

scandal
labyrinth
member
moral values
gossip
pyramid

a He agreed with their _____, and never wanted to seem different from them.
b As long as a _____ of a well-known family is supported by that family, that person should be accepted by the others.
c Listening to all this _____, Newland Archer suddenly wanted to sit with the ladies.
d The _____ would damage her family.
e "Is New York such a _____? I thought it was straight up and down like Fifth Avenue, with all the streets numbered."
f The New York of that time was a small _____ of different types of people.

8 People are addressed in different ways in the story. Write the titles in the correct box (MALE or FEMALE) and then find out when they should be used.

| Mr | Mrs | Miss | Madame |
| Monsieur | Count | Countess | Duke |

MALE

FEMALE

9 Put the words below in the order that they usually happen in relationships (1-6).

_____ a marriage

_____ b proposal

_____ c wedding

_____ d announcement

_____ e honeymoon

_____ f engagement

10 Use some of the words from Exercise **9** to complete the sentences.

a I really don't want a long _____.

b He could only hope that the first six months of _____ were always the most difficult.

c He hoped to convince her of an earlier _____.

d They went on a three-month _____ in Europe.

11 Make sentences using the words left out in Exercise **10**.

1. The opera

On a January evening in the early 1870s, the most elegant families of New York gathered at the Academy of Music. They happily filled the blue and gold boxes of this small and uncomfortable building, very much loved by conservative[1] New Yorkers.

When Newland Archer opened the door at the back of the box he shared with his friends, the opera had already begun. He was not worried about his late arrival. It was not "the thing" to arrive early at the opera, and what was or was not the thing was important to Newland Archer.

Directly opposite him was the box of old Mrs Manson Mingott. Although the old lady had grown too large to come to the theater, her daughter, Mrs Welland, and daughter-in-law, Mrs Lovell Mingott, were there. With these two ladies sat a young girl in a white dress with the bouquet of lilies-of-the-valley[2] on her knee. She was May Welland, his sweetheart, the future Mrs Newland Archer.

---

1 conservative [kən`sɜvətɪv] (a.) 保守的
2 lily-of-the-valley 歐鈴蘭

4

Newland looked at his future wife, thinking of the books they would read together and admiring her innocence. He wanted her to be clever and witty[1] and charming. And if he were honest he wished her to be as interesting as that married woman he had been in love with for two years, without any of that woman's unhappiness of course.

The Opera

- Discuss what you know about operas with a partner.
- Can you name any operas?

Newland Archer thought of himself as superior[2] to the other men in the New York upper class. He had read more, thought more and seen more of the world than any of them. However, he didn't want to appear different, so he agreed with their moral values on all things.

As Archer was standing there thinking about these things, the other men in the box were talking about the lady who was sitting with May and her family. Archer realized they were talking about May Welland's cousin, the "poor Ellen Olenska", who had just returned from Europe.

5

　She was the black sheep[3] of the family, and it surprised Archer that the Mingotts presented her in public at the opera. It was obvious that old Mrs Mingott, the head of the family, dared[4] to do anything she wanted.

　Still, Archer hated to think that his fiancée[5] could be seen with a woman who had just left her husband, even if that husband was a brute[6]. They also said that Countess Olenska had run away with her husband's secretary and then lived alone in Venice.

　Listening to all this gossip[7], Newland Archer suddenly wanted to sit with the ladies and show the world that he was engaged to May and that he supported her family.

Ellen Olenska

- What is the gossip about Ellen Olenska?
- How do you think she feels?

1　witty [ˋwɪtɪ] (a.) 風趣的
2　superior [səˋpɪrɪɚ]
　　(a.) 較好的；較優秀的
3　black sheep 害群之馬；敗類

4　dare [dɛr] (v.) 竟敢
5　fiancée [ˌfiənˋse] (n.) 未婚妻
6　brute [brut] (n.) 殘暴的人
7　gossip [ˋɡɑsəp] (n.) 閒話；八卦

2. The engagement

[6]   It always happened the same way. After the first night of the opera there was a ball at the Beauforts'. Their house was one of the few in New York with a ballroom. Both their house and their lifestyle were luxurious, and this compensated[1] for their shameful[2] past. Mrs Regina Beaufort came from an honorable[3] but now poor family in the South, and her husband, Julius Beaufort, was an agreeable hospitable[4] Englishman with mysterious secrets. His marriage to Regina brought him acceptance in New York society, but it did not bring him respect.

After the opera, Archer did not go back to his club with the other young men, but he walked along Fifth Avenue[5] before turning back in the direction of the Beauforts'. Archer was nervous. He was afraid that the Mingotts would bring Countess Olenska to the ball.

When Archer arrived, May Welland was standing at the side of the ballroom, holding her bouquet of lilies-of-the-valley in her hand. She was surrounded[6] by a group of happily laughing friends, who were all delighted to hear about her engagement.

Society

- In 1870s New York society, wealth and family are very important. Is it the same today?
- Why? Why not?

Newland walked over and led May onto the dance floor. Then when the music was over they went into the conservatory[7] together.

"You see I did as you asked me to," she said.

"I wish it hadn't had to be at a ball."

"Yes, I know." She glanced at him understandingly. "But after all, even here we're alone together, aren't we?"

"Oh, dearest, always!" Archer cried.

"Did you tell my cousin Ellen?" she asked.

"No, I didn't have the chance," he lied.

She looked disappointed. "You must, then, for I didn't either."

"But I haven't seen her yet. Has she come?" Archer asked.

1 compensate [ˈkɑmpənˌset] (v.) 補償
2 shameful [ˈʃemfəl] (a.) 不體面的
3 honorable [ˈɑnərəbl] (a.) 可尊敬的
4 hospitable [ˈhɑspɪtəbl] (a.) 好客的
5 avenue [ˈævəˌnju] (n.) 大街
6 surround [səˈraʊnd] (v.) 圍繞
7 conservatory [kənˈsɝvəˌtorɪ] (n.) 溫室

"No. At the last minute she decided not to. She said her dress wasn't smart enough for a ball, so my aunt had to take her home," May answered.

Of course, Archer knew the real reason for her cousin not coming to the ball. However, he didn't want his fiancée to know that he was aware of poor Ellen Olenska's bad reputation[1].

May and Newland

- Are they happy together? What makes you think so?

The next day, the young couple made the first of the usual betrothal[2] visits. Mrs Manson Mingott was a respected old lady and most of the New York families were related to her. It was her honor to be the first to give the couple her blessing.

Mrs Mingott lived in a cream-colored stone house near Central Park. As she got heavier, it became impossible for her to go up and downstairs, so she decided to sleep on the ground floor of her house.

1 reputation [ˌrɛpjəˈteʃən] (n.) 聲譽
2 betrothal [bɪˈtroθəl] (n.) 訂婚

It was unusual to see into someone's bedroom from the sitting room, but her visitors were fascinated[1] by this arrangement. She spent most of her time by the window of her sitting room, watching calmly for life and fashion to arrive at her door.

"And when is the wedding?" asked Mrs Mingott, looking at the couple.

"As soon as possible, if you support me," replied Archer.

"We must give them time to get to know each other a little better, mamma," said Mrs Welland.

"Know each other? Nonsense! Everybody in New York has always known everybody. Get married before Lent[2]! And I want to host[3] the wedding-breakfast."

The visit was ending when Countess Olenska arrived with Julius Beaufort. The Countess looked at Archer with a smile.

"Of course you know already about May and me," he said.

"Of course I know; yes. And I'm so glad," she answered, holding out her hand. "Goodbye. Come and see me some day," she said, still looking at Archer.

---

1 fascinated [ˈfæsṇˌetɪd] (a.) 著迷的
2 Lent [lɛnt] (n.) 四旬齋；大齋期（復活節前的四十天）
3 host [host] (v.) (n.) 主人

3. The Archers

(10) The next evening, old Mr Sillerton Jackson dined with the Archers. Mrs Archer and her daughter Janey were both shy women. Mother and daughter adored each other and respected their son and brother, and Newland Archer loved them both dearly. Whenever Mrs Archer wanted to know about anything in the life of New York's great families, she asked Mr Jackson to dine.

The city was divided into two types of great families. There were the Mingotts and Mansons, who cared about eating and clothes and money, and the Archer-Newland-van-der-Luyden tribe[1], who loved travel, horticulture[2] and the best fiction.

"And Newland's new cousin, Countess Olenska? Was she at the ball, too?" asked Mrs Archer.

"No, she was not at the ball," Mr Jackson replied.

"Perhaps the Beauforts don't know her," Janey suggested.

"Mrs Beaufort may not, but Mr Beaufort certainly does. They were seen walking on Fifth Avenue this afternoon," Mr Jackson said.

"Anyway, it was best for her not to go to the ball," Mrs Archer said, showing her disapproval[3].

"May said that she wanted to go, but then decided that her dress wasn't smart enough," Archer commented.

"Poor Ellen, she is so different from us," Mrs Archer added.

"Why shouldn't she be different if she chooses? Just because she made a bad marriage, does not mean that she should be punished," replied her son angrily.

"That, I suppose," said Mr Jackson, "is the opinion of the Mingott family."

The young man's face turned red. "I didn't have to wait for their opinion, if that's what you mean, sir. Madame Olenska has had an unhappy life, but she belongs to us."

"I hear she wants to get a divorce," said Janey.

"I hope she will!" Archer exclaimed.

A few days later, the unthinkable happened. Mrs Mingott sent out invitations for a formal dinner to meet Countess Olenska. Forty-eight hours later everyone had refused the invitation except the Beauforts and old Mr Jackson and his sister.

---

1 tribe [traɪb] (n.) 族群；部落
2 horticulture [ˈhɔrtɪˌkʌltʃɚ] (n.) 園藝
3 disapproval [ˌdɪsəˈpruvl] (n.) 不贊同；不認同

The blow[1] was unexpected, but the Mingotts reacted to it elegantly[2]. They contacted the Archers and Mrs Archer decided to visit the van der Luydens.

The New York of that time was a small pyramid of different types of people. At the bottom were the plain[3] respectable families. Then there were families like the Mingotts and the Newlands. Most people imagined them to be at the top of the pyramid, but they knew they were not. Just three families made up the aristocracy[4] of New York, and the van der Luydens, who were related to the Archers, were one of them.

"We are going to talk to them because of May, and also because, if we don't all stand together, there'll be no such thing as Society left," said Archer's mother.

"It's the principle that I dislike," said Mr van der Luyden. "As long as a member of a well-known family is supported by that family, that person should be accepted by the others. I had no idea," Mr van der Luyden continued, "that things had come to such a pass[5]"

Then, with his wife's approval[6], he decided to invite Countess Olenska to a dinner that they were organizing for the Duke of St. Austrey and a few selected friends.

---

1 blow [blo] (n.) 衝擊；風暴
2 elegantly [ˈɛləɡəntlɪ] (adv.) 優雅地
3 plain [plen] (a.) 平凡的
4 aristocracy [ˌærəsˈtɑkrəsɪ] (n.) 貴族
5 things has come to such a pass 如今走到了這般田地
6 approval [əˈpruvl] (n.) 贊成；同意

On the night of the dinner, Countess Olenska arrived late at the van der Luydens', but she entered the drawing room without any hurry or embarrassment. When she paused in the middle of the room, Archer noticed her mysterious beauty and simple behavior. She was quiet in her movements and voice, and not as stylish as everyone had expected her to be.

The van der Luydens had done their best to convey[1] the importance of the evening. All the ladies were wearing diamond necklaces and elegant dresses, except for the two main guests, the Duke of St. Austrey and Countess Olenska, who both looked less conspicuous[2] than the others.

After dinner the Countess walked across the drawing room and sat down at Archer's side, even though it was not customary[3] for women to choose to sit beside a man.

"I want you to talk to me about May," she said. "She is beautiful and intelligent. Are you very much in love with her?"

Newland Archer reddened and laughed. "As much as a man can be."

"Ah, it's really and truly a romance, then. It was not in the least arranged."

"Have you forgotten? In our country we don't allow our marriages to be arranged for us."

1 convey [kən`ve] (v.) 傳達
2 conspicuous [kən`spɪkjuəs] (a.) 顯著的
3 customary [`kʌstəm͵ɛrɪ] (a.) 慣常的

"Sorry, I forgot. I don't always remember that things are different here," the Countess replied.

"I'm so sorry. But you are among friends here, you know," Archer said.

"Yes, I know. That's why I came home."

As they were talking, Mr van der Luyden interrupted them.

"Tomorrow, then, after five, I shall expect you," the Countess told Archer as he was leaving.

"Tomorrow." Archer heard himself repeating the word, although they had not discussed a meeting before.

4. The visit

(15) At half past five Newland Archer arrived at Countess Olenska's house. It was a strange quarter of New York to live in. Her neighbors were dressmakers, journalists and writers. The Countess was out when he arrived but her maid[1] welcomed him and left him in the drawing room to wait.

After some time, the Countess arrived home accompanied by Julius Beaufort, who left immediately. When she entered the room, she showed no surprise.

"How do you like my funny[1] house?" she asked. "To me it's like heaven."

"You've arranged it delightfully," he replied.

"Oh, it's a poor little place. My family despises[2] it." Ellen replied and sat down by the fire.

"I was afraid you'd forgotten the hour," Archer added, referring to the fact that she was late.

"Why? Have you waited long? Mr Beaufort took me to see a number of houses. They told me I must move although this street seems fine to me."

"It's not fashionable," answered Archer.

"Do you think fashion is so important? I just want to feel loved and safe, but my family is a little angry with me for living here alone."

Funny House

1. What is important to Ellen about where she lives?
2. What is important to Ellen's family?
3. What is important to you about where you live?

"I think I understand how you feel," he said. "Still, your family can advise you; explain differences; show you the way."

"Is New York such a labyrinth? I thought it was straight up and down like Fifth Avenue, with all the streets numbered."

"Everything may be labeled, but not everyone." Archer wanted to take this opportunity[3] to warn her about Beaufort.

"There are only two people here who make me feel as if they understand me and explain things to me. You and Mr Beaufort," Ellen replied.

"I understand. But don't forget your old friends. They want to help you, too," he answered kindly.

---

1 funny [ˈfʌnɪ] (a.) 奇怪的
2 despise [dɪˈspaɪz] (v.) 看不起
3 opportunity [ˌɑpəˈtjunətɪ] (n.) 機會

Ellen sighed. "Oh, I know! But they only want to help when they don't hear anything unpleasant about me. Does no one want to know the truth here, Mr Archer? The real loneliness is living among all these kind people who only want you to pretend[1]!" She lifted her hands to her face and started to cry.

"Oh, don't, Ellen," he said and went over to her.

"Does no one cry here, either?" she asked.

Mr Beaufort

- Why does Archer want to warn Ellen about Mr Beaufort?

Archer left the house and walked into the cold winter night. He went straight to the florist's[2] to send May her daily box of lilies-of-the-valley which he had forgotten about that morning.

While he was writing the card for May, he noticed a cluster[3] of yellow roses, and with a sudden gesture, he sent them to Countess Olenska.

---

1 pretend [prɪˈtɛnd] (v.) 假裝
2 the florist's 花店
3 cluster [ˈklʌstɚ] (n.) 束；簇

The next day he persuaded[1] May to go for a walk in the park after lunch.

"It's so wonderful to wake up every morning to the smell of lilies-of-the-valley in my room!" she said.

"Yesterday they came late. I didn't have time in the morning," Archer replied.

"But you always remember."

"I sent some flowers to your cousin Ellen, too. Was that right?"

"How kind of you! But she didn't mention[2] it at lunch today. She only mentioned the nice flowers she got from Mr Beaufort and Mr van der Luyden."

"Oh, I expect mine were overshadowed[3] by Beaufort's," said Archer irritably.

Then, to distract himself, Archer began to talk of their future, and Mrs Welland's hope for a long engagement. Archer wanted nothing more than to marry May as soon as possible. But May was a conventional[4] young woman and wanted to take things more slowly.

Archer

- How does Archer feel?
- Why is he irritated?

5. The divorce

Two weeks later, Newland Archer was summoned by Mr Letterblair, the head of the law firm where he worked. He learnt that Countess Olenska wished to get divorced from her husband. This worried the whole Mingott family, and they sought[5] professional advice in order to stop the divorce from happening.

Archer didn't agree with the idea of divorce and he felt annoyed that he was being asked to deal with the case. However, when he heard that both the Mingotts and the Wellands wanted him, he reluctantly[6] accepted the task.

After reading the legal papers, Newland Archer decided that he had to see Madame Olenska if he wanted to understand her side of the story. So he wrote a message to the Countess, asking at what time the next day she could receive him. She replied quickly saying that he would find her alone that evening after dinner.

---

1 persuade [pɚˋswed] (v.) 說服
2 mention [ˋmɛnʃən] (v.) 提及；說起
3 overshadow [͵ovɚˋʃædo] (v.) 使相形見拙
4 conventional [kənˋvɛnʃənl] (a.) 傳統式的；習慣的
5 seek [sik] (v.) 尋求（動詞三態：seek–sought–sought）
6 reluctantly [rɪˋlʌktəntlɪ] (adv.) 不情願地

When Nastasia, Countess Olenska's maid, opened the door, she smiled mysteriously. Julius Beaufort was visiting the Countess, and although Archer had not told Ellen that he wished to see her privately, he was still annoyed.

"Three whole days at cold Skuytercliff!" Beaufort was talking in his loud voice as Archer entered.

They were discussing Madame Olenska's visit to the van der Luyden country house.

"Why? Is the house so cold?" she asked.

"No, but the missus[1] is. You should stay here and come with me to Delmonico's next Sunday and meet artists and other happy people."

"That sounds interesting! I have met only one artist since I've been here," Ellen replied. "May I think it over[2], and write to you tomorrow morning?"

"Why not now?" Beaufort seemed impatient.

"Because I still have to talk business with Mr Archer."

Beaufort left and Madame Olenska and Archer continued talking in the drawing room.

"I'm here to talk about your case with Mr Letterblair," he said. "I've looked through the papers you gave to him."

"Oh, did you? You know, I want to be free; I want to wipe out[3] all the past," she replied passionately.

"I understand that."

"Then you'll help me?"

"First, perhaps I should know a little more."

"It was a horrible marriage," Ellen replied.

Archer tried to explain to her that even if she wanted her freedom back, a divorce would be unpleasant to their families. Although a divorce was legally possible in America, New York society did not favor it. The scandal[4] would damage her family.

The Countess sadly accepted Archer's advice and promised him that she would do whatever he wished.

The next evening at the theater, Archer met Madame Olenska once more.

"Do you think he will send her yellow roses tomorrow morning?" Ellen asked, turning to Archer and pointing to the lovers on the stage.

Archer's face turned red. He had visited Madame Olenska twice, and each time he had sent her a box of yellow roses, and each time without a card. She had never mentioned them before and he had thought she didn't know that he was the sender. The thought filled him with pleasure.

1   missus [ˈmɪsəs] (n.)〔舊〕妻子
2   think over 仔細考慮
3   wipe out 除去或取消某事物
4   scandal [ˈskændl] (n.) 醜聞

6. At Skuytercliff

The next morning, Archer searched the city for yellow roses without any success.

When he got to the office he sent a note by messenger[1] to Madame Olenska, asking if he might visit her that afternoon. But she replied three days later from Skuytercliff where she was staying with the van der Luydens.

> I ran away after I saw you at the play, and these kind friends have taken me in. I wanted to be quiet and think things over. You were right in telling me how kind they were; I feel so safe here. I wish that you were with us.
>
> Yours sincerely,
> Ellen

He felt disappointed to learn that Madame Olenska was away, and then immediately remembered that he had an invitation to spend the weekend with some friends, the Chiverses, only a few miles from Skuytercliff.

23   He arrived there on Friday evening, and on Saturday he went through all the usual activities of a weekend in the country. He went out on the ice-boat, and then to the farm to see the horses. After tea he talked in a corner with some other guests.

But on Sunday after lunch, he drove over to Skuytercliff and, as Ellen wasn't in, he decided to walk towards the village in the hope of meeting her.

Presently[2], he caught sight of a slight[3] figure[4] in a red cloak; it was her!

"Ah, you've come!" she said.

"I came to see what you were running away from," he laughed.

"I knew you'd come!" she smiled back at him.

"It was because I got your note. Ellen, why don't you tell me what's happened?"

As they were walking past the van der Luydens' house, they noticed that the door was open.

Madame Olenska dropped her red cloak and sat down on one of the chairs. Archer leaned against the chimney and looked at her.

---

1   messenger [ˈmɛsn̩dʒɚ] (n.) 信差
2   presently [ˈprɛzn̩tlɪ] (adv.) 一會兒
3   slight [slaɪt] (a.) 細長的
4   figure [ˈfɪgjɚ] (n.) 體形

(24) "You're laughing now, but when you wrote to me you were unhappy," he said.

"Yes, but I can't feel unhappy when you're here," she answered.

For a long moment she was silent. In that moment Archer imagined her walking behind him and throwing her arms around his neck. While he waited for this to happen, he saw someone walking towards the house. It was Julius Beaufort.

Julius Beaufort

- Think back. On what other occasions has Julius Beaufort been with Madame Olenska?
- How did Archer react?
- What do you think will happen next?

Madame Olenska quickly moved to Archer's side, slipping[1] her hand into his.

"So, you're running from him?" Archer asked rudely[2].

"I didn't know he was here," Madame Olenska answered. Archer then walked to the front door and threw it open to welcome Beaufort.

"Hallo, Beaufort—this way! Madame Olenska was expecting you," he said as he left.

---

1 slip [slɪp] (v.) 滑動
2 rudely [ˋrudlɪ] (adv.) 無禮地

[25] Back in New York, the next two or three days dragged by[1] heavily. He heard nothing of Countess Olenska and though he saw Beaufort at the club they didn't speak.

On the fourth evening, he received a message from her, which said:

> *Come late tomorrow: I must explain to you.*
>
> *Ellen.*

After dinner he went to a play. When he returned home, after midnight, he reread the message slowly a few times. He did not know how to answer.

When morning came, he decided to pack his bag and jump on a boat for St. Augustine in Florida, where May and her family were spending the winter months.

7. A short engagement

26

When Archer walked down the sandy main street of St. Augustine to the house which had been pointed out to him as Mr Welland's, and saw May standing under a magnolia[2] tree with the sun in her hair, he wondered why he had waited so long to come.

"Newland, has anything happened?" May looked surprised to see her fiancé there.

"Yes. I had to see you," he answered.

And her happy blushes took the chill[3] from her surprise.

"Tell me what you do all day," he said.

"We go swimming, sailing and riding, sometimes dancing. A few pleasant people from Philadelphia and Baltimore were picnicking at the inn, and sometimes I play tennis."

All this kept her very busy, she said. She had not had time to read the little book that Archer had sent her the week before, but how could she, when she was learning a poem by heart[4]?

¹ drag by 慢慢過去
² magnolia [mæɡˈnolɪə] (n.) 木蘭
³ chill [tʃɪl] (n.) 冷淡；寒冷
⁴ by heart 背下來地

All through his stay, Archer hoped to convince[1] May of an earlier wedding. On the day before his departure[2], he talked to her again.

"We could be in Europe in spring and see the Easter ceremonies[3] in Seville," he said.

"Easter in Seville? And it will be Lent next week!" she laughed.

"We could be married soon after Easter and sail at the end of April. I know I could arrange it at the office."

She smiled at the possibility.

"Why should we wait another year? Look at me, dear! Don't you understand how much I want you for my wife?" Archer was suddenly impatient.

"I'm not sure if I understand," she said. "Is it because you're not certain of your feelings for me?"

"Oh, maybe, I don't know," he answered angrily.

"Is there someone else? Let's talk frankly[4], Newland. Sometimes I've felt a difference in you, especially since our engagement has been announced."

"Dear! What madness!" Archer did not like what she was saying.

"If it isn't true, it should be fine to talk about it. Or even if it is true, why shouldn't we speak about it? You might have made a mistake."

1 convince [kənˈvɪns] (v.) 說服
2 departure [dɪˈpɑrtʃɚ] (n.) 離開
3 ceremony [ˈsɛrəˌmonɪ] (n.) 典禮
4 frankly [ˈfræŋklɪ] (adv.) 坦白地

"Would I ask you to marry me if I had made a mistake?" he answered.

"People said there was someone else for you a few years ago. And once I saw you sitting with this woman on the veranda[1] at a dance. When she came back into the house her face was sad, and I felt sorry for her." May talked patiently.

"Are you worried about that? If only you knew the truth!"

"Is there a truth I don't know?"

"I mean the truth about this old story you speak of."

"Newland, I couldn't be happy if it meant hurting somebody else. We could not build a life like that. And if you have made promises to this other person, don't give her up because of me!"

"There are no promises, May. There is no one and nothing between us," Newland answered.

When Archer returned to New York, he had many messages for old Mrs Mingott. The old lady was grateful to him for persuading Countess Olenska to give up the idea of a divorce. She was even happier to hear that he had rushed down to St. Augustine to see May.

"Were they all surprised when you arrived? How did May react?" she asked.

"I wanted her to promise me that we could get married in April. Why should we waste another year?" complained Archer.

"Ah, these Mingotts! They are all the same! No, not one of them wants to be different; they're all scared of it. Not one of my children takes after[2] me, but my little Ellen. Now, why didn't you marry my little Ellen?"

"Well, she wasn't there to be married," Archer laughed.

"And now it's too late; her life is finished," replied Mrs Mingott.

"Can't I convince you to use your influence with the Wellands, Mrs Mingott? I really don't want a long engagement," asked Archer.

"I can see that," Mrs Mingott replied.

Old Mrs Mingott

- What is Mrs Mingott like? Write a list of adjectives. Go back to pages 23 and 25 for more clues.

At that moment, Madame Olenska walked in with a smile.

"I was asking him why he didn't marry you, my dear Ellen."

Madame Olenska looked at Archer, still smiling. "And what did he answer?"

"My dear, I'll let you find that out! He's been down to Florida to see his sweetheart."

---

1   veranda [vəˈrændə] (n.) 陽臺
2   take after 相似

"Yes, I know," answered Ellen, still looking at Archer. "I went to see your mother to ask where you'd gone. I sent a note that you never answered, and I was afraid you were ill. And of course when you were in Florida, you never thought of me again!" said Ellen to Archer.

Archer got up to leave, and Ellen walked with him to the door.

"When can I see you again?" he asked.

"Whenever you like, but it must be soon if you want to see the little house again. I am moving next week," she replied.

"Tomorrow evening?" asked Archer.

She nodded[1]. "Tomorrow, yes. But come early. I'm going out in the evening."

Note

- What did Ellen's note say? Check on page 50.

---

1 nod [nɑd] (v.) 點頭表示
2 on one's own terms 依自己的意願
3 shimmering [ˋʃɪmərɪŋ] (a.) 閃爍的

8. Another visit to Countess Olenska

The next day, Archer heard that Ellen's husband, the Count, had sent a letter to her saying she could go back to him on her own terms². He was shocked and hated the idea, but it reminded him that Ellen was still the Count's wife.

When Archer went to see her, she appeared in a beautiful shimmering³ dress. As soon as she walked into the drawing room, she noticed a large bouquet of flowers that upset her. They were from her husband.

She immediately called for Nastasia, and sent the flowers to one of her neighbors as a surprise.

Flowers

- Flowers are important in this story. Write a list of who has sent flowers to whom so far.
- What do you think they mean in each example?

"What have you heard about me?" she asked Archer.

"Well, I've heard that Count Olenski wants you to go back to him. I've heard about a letter."

"After all, it is not a surprise," she replied after some silence. "Many cruel things have been believed of me." She smiled a little. "And you, Newland, you're horribly nervous. You also have your own troubles. I know you think that May's family does not support your early marriage, and of course I agree with you. In Europe people don't understand our long American engagements."

"Yes, I went south to ask May to marry me after Easter. There's no reason why we shouldn't be married then."

"And May adores you. It is strange that you could not convince her."

"We had our first honest talk. She thinks it is a bad sign that I am impatient. She also thinks it means that I can't trust myself. She thinks that I want to marry her to get away[1] from someone that I love more."

"But if she thinks that, why isn't she in a hurry, too?" Ellen asked.

"She wants the long engagement to give me time . . ."

"Time to leave her for another woman?"

"If that's what I want."

"That IS noble," Ellen said.

"Yes. But it's ridiculous," answered Archer.

"Why is it ridiculous? You don't love another woman?"

"No. Because I don't mean to marry anyone else."

---

1 get away 離開

"Does this other woman love you?" asked Ellen.

"There is another woman, but not the one May thinks."

Ellen Olenska did not answer, did not move.

After a moment he sat down beside her and took her hand.

"You are the woman I would have married if it had been possible for us."

"You have made it impossible for us to be together," replied Ellen.

"I have made it impossible?"

"You convinced me to give up the idea of the divorce to save our family from the scandal! And because my family was going to be your family, I did what you told me. I did it all for you!" Ellen was almost crying.

"At least I loved you," he confessed[1].

He went over to her and kissed her. Simply touching her made everything so simple.

She gave him back all his kisses, but after a moment she moved away from him.

"You have changed my life," he said to Ellen.

"No, no! You're engaged to May, and I'm married."

"Nonsense! We cannot lie to other people or to ourselves. How can I marry May after this?"

"I hope you are not going to ask May that question," Ellen replied.

"It's too late to do anything else," Archer answered.

34 "You have done so much for me," said Ellen. "You went to the van der Luydens because people refused to meet me at dinner. You announced your engagement at the Beaufort ball so there would be two families to stand by[2] me."

At that moment they were interrupted by Nastasia, who came in carrying a telegram[3]. It was addressed to the Countess and had been sent from St. Augustine.

WESTERN UNION TELEGRAPH COMPANY

To: *Countess Ellen Olenska*

By Telegraph, from: *St. Augustine*

Granny's telegram successful. Papa and Mamma agree marriage after Easter. Am telegraphing Newland. Am too happy for words and love you dearly. Your grateful May.

---

1 confess [kənˋfɛs] (v.) 坦白；承認
2 stand by 支持
3 telegram [ˋtɛləˏgræm] (n.) 電報

　Half an hour later, when Archer arrived home, he found a similar envelope. The message inside the envelope was also from May.

WESTERN UNION TELEGRAPH COMPANY

To: *Newland Archer*

By Telegraph, from: *St. Augustine*

Parents consent[1] wedding. Tuesday after Easter. At twelve. Grace Church. Eight bridesmaids. Please see Rector. So happy. love May.

Archer started trembling[2] and checking his diary. His sister appeared to see what was happening.

"Newland! I hope there's no bad news in that telegram."

"Nothing's the matter, except that I'm going to be married in a month."

And he threw back his head with a long laugh.

9. The wedding

The day was fresh, with a lively spring wind full of dust. Newland Archer stood waiting for his bride on the steps of Grace Church.

He had fulfilled all his obligations[3] before the wedding: flowers for the bridesmaids, a scarf pin[4] for the best man, thank-you notes for the gifts and money for the bishop[5]. Everything was equally easy—or equally painful—in the path he was committed[6] to tread[7].

Handel's March[8] rang out and the bridegroom looked around the church.

"It's just like a first night at the opera," he thought, recognizing all the same faces.

He suddenly remembered that once he had thought weddings to be unimportant. Yet now the preparations for his own marriage seemed like a parody[9] of life.

1 consent [kən'sɛnt] (v.) 贊同
2 tremble ['trɛmbl̩] (v.) 顫抖
3 obligation [ˌɑbləˈgeʃən] (n.) 義務
4 scarf pin 圍巾針

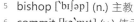

5 bishop ['bɪʃəp] (n.) 主教
6 commit [kəˈmɪt] (v.) 使承擔義務；使做出保證
7 tread [trɛd] (v.) 踏
8 Handel's March 韓德爾的結婚進行曲
9 parody ['pærədɪ] (n.) 滑稽模仿作品

37   "Real people are living somewhere, and real things are happening to them," he thought.

"Newland, she's here!" the best man whispered.

Archer opened his eyes (were they really shut?) and in a moment May was beside him. Then the ring was on her finger and they were walking out of the church towards the carriage[1] that would take them to Mrs Mingott's and the wedding breakfast. Archer felt himself falling deeper and deeper into a black abyss[2] while he talked happily to his bride.

After the wedding breakfast, the couple went to the station and set off[3] towards Rhineback where they were staying for their wedding night. Archer looked at May: she was still the simple girl of yesterday and he felt like a stranger.

"I do wish Ellen had been there," she said suddenly, and Archer felt his world tumble[4] around him.

---

1 carriage [ˈkærɪdʒ] (n.) 馬車
2 abyss [əˈbɪs] (n.) 深淵
3 set off 啟程
4 tumble [ˈtʌmbl̩] (v.) 墜落；崩落

10. The honeymoon[1]

The Newland Archers set off on a three-month honeymoon to Europe. After a month in Paris visiting dressmakers, May wanted to go swimming and mountaineering in Switzerland, so they went. Then they stopped at a little place on the Normandy coast before arriving in London. Traveling interested May less than Newland had expected, and she was looking forward to returning home.

In the meantime, Archer had lost his enthusiasm about marriage. But it was easier to conform[2] and treat May the same way as all his friends treated their wives. He knew that whatever happened, she would always be loyal to him, and he promised to be the same.

Marriage

- What did Archer think about marriage at the start of the story?
- What does he think now?
- What has changed?

---

1 honeymoon [ˈhʌnɪˌmun] (n.) 蜜月
2 conform [kənˈfɔrm] (v.) 遵從

Before they left London, Newland and May were invited to dine with Mrs Carfry, an old friend of Newland's mother.

"There'll probably be no one at Mrs Carfry's," said Archer as they drove across London. "And you've made yourself too beautiful!"

"I don't want them to think that we dress like savages[3]," May replied scornfully[4].

Archer had been right. It was a small party and after dinner the ladies went into the drawing-room leaving Archer to talk with Monsieur Rivière, the Carfrys' French tutor. They spoke about books and culture and intellectual[5] freedom. Archer felt new air in his lungs.

"We had an awfully good talk. That young Frenchman is an interesting fellow[6]. We talked about books and things," he told May in the carriage on the way home.

"The Frenchman? Wasn't he terribly common?" exclaimed May. "I suppose I wouldn't have known if he was clever," she added.

Archer disliked her use of "common" and "clever" and he was beginning to fear his tendency[7] to notice things he disliked in her.

"Ah, then I won't ask him to dine!" he replied with a laugh.

He was shocked to think that this was now his future. He could only hope that the first six months of marriage were always the most difficult. After that life should become easier.

---

3 savage [ˋsævɪdʒ] (n.) 粗魯的人;野蠻人
4 scornfully [ˋskɔrnfəlɪ] (adv.) 輕蔑地
5 intellectual [ˌɪntlˋɛktʃuəl] (a.) 智性的;知識的

6 fellow [ˋfɛlo] (n.) 傢伙
7 tendency [ˋtɛndənsɪ]
    (n.) 傾向

11. The archery competition[1]

As the couple settled in their new life, Newland could not say that he had made a mistake by marrying May. She was beautiful and popular and the most reasonable[2] of wives. He arranged his new library as he wished, spent time with his old friends again, worked in the law office and dined out or entertained friends at home.

Their life was pleasant, and he thought of his feelings towards Countess Olenska as a moment of madness, and she remained in his memory as the last in a line of ghosts.

He was thinking about all of these things as he was standing on the veranda of the Beaufort house, where the annual[3] Newport Archery[4] competition was held in August. May was about to win the competition—a sport as popular as croquet[5]. Archery was considered to be a classic and elegant sport and the day of the competition was an important social occasion for New York families.

As Newland stood watching the competition, he overheard his host talk about May's victory.

"That's the only kind of target she'll ever hit," said Beaufort, and it made Archer very angry.

He was afraid that he might find out that there was only emptiness behind the curtain of May's kindness and serenity[6]. He felt that she had never lifted the curtain. She was simple and nice to everyone, and no one could ever be jealous of her.

May

- **What is May like?**
- **What do you think Archer means by "lifting the curtain"?**

As they were driving home after the archery competition, May suddenly proposed a visit to her grandmother, to tell her that she had won the first prize.

Mrs Mingott admired the diamond arrow that May had won, and pinched[7] May's arm saying, "You must leave it for your eldest girl."

May blushed[8] at the idea of having children, and they all ended up laughing together at the embarrassment[9].

---

1 competition [ˌkɑmpəˈtɪʃən] (n.) 競賽
2 reasonable [ˈriznəbl̩] (a.) 通情達理的
3 annual [ˈænjuəl] (a.) 年度的
4 archery [ˈɑrtʃərɪ] (n.) 箭術
5 croquet [kroˈke] (n.) 槌球
6 serenity [səˈrɛnətɪ] (n.) 沉著
7 pinch [pɪntʃ] (v.) 捏；擰
8 blush [blʌʃ] (v.) 臉紅
9 embarrassment [ɪmˈbærəsmənt] (n.) 困窘

During their visit they learnt that Madame Olenska was also there. She had come over from Portsmouth, where she was staying with a family called the Blenkers, to spend the day with Mrs Mingott.

When Mrs Mingott called for Ellen, the maid informed her that she had gone down the shore path[1].

"Run down and fetch her, Newland," said Mrs Mingott.

Archer stood up as if in a dream. Although he had heard about Ellen's life since his marriage to May, she became a living presence to him again only on this day of the archery competition.

As If in a Dream

- What do you think this means?
- What are Archer's feelings towards Ellen?

12. At the pier

Archer walked down the path[1] and saw the wooden pier[2] with the summer house at the end of it. A woman with her back to the shore was standing there, leaning against the rail[3]. It was Ellen.

Neither Archer, nor Ellen moved, and for a long moment he stood on the bank, gazing[4] at the sea. She was looking out to sea, watching the yachts, sailboats and fishing boats. There was a sailboat gliding[5] through the channel between Lime Rock lighthouse and the shore.

Archer thought, "If she doesn't turn before the sail crosses the Lime Rock light, I'll go back."

She did not move. He turned and walked up the hill.

Archer

- Why doesn't Archer speak to Ellen?
- How does he feel?

---

1 path [pæθ] (n.) 小徑
2 pier [pɪr] (n.) 凸式碼頭

3 rail [rel] (n.) 欄杆
4 gaze [gez] (v.) 凝視；注視
5 glide [glaɪd] (v.) 滑行

44   Archer wasn't sure if he wanted to see Ellen again, but he could not stop thinking about her. The memory of her on the beach felt closer to him than the life he was living.

He now felt a strong desire to see where she was living. When a late summer party was organized by the Sillertons for the Blenkers, he realized he had the chance to satisfy his curiosity. He felt that if he could see the spot of earth that she had walked on, the world might seem less empty.

He planned to go over to the Blenkers on the day of the party, when there was nobody at home. He would say he was interested in buying a horse from a farm close by.

When the day came, it was perfect. He arrived and stood by the gate, happy to take in[1] the scene. Then he walked towards the garden. There was something brightly colored in the summer house. It looked like a pink parasol[2], and it drew him like a magnet. He was sure that it was Ellen's.

He picked it up and lifted it close to his face to smell it. He heard someone behind him and waited for Ellen's voice and touch. But it was one of the Blenker girls! She was friendly but also surprised to find Archer in the garden.

1 take in 慢慢地觀賞
2 parasol [ˈpærəˌsɔl] (n.) 陽傘

"Didn't you know that the Sillertons are having a garden party for all of us this afternoon?" she asked. "I couldn't go as I have a sore throat."

When Archer asked if Madame Olenska had also gone there, Miss Blenker looked at him with surprise.

"Madame Olenska's been called away! A telegram came from Boston, and she said she might be gone for two days."

"I'm going to Boston tomorrow. Do you know where . . .?"

"Of course! She's staying at the Parker House," and she continued to talk about Ellen.

Archer stopped listening.

13. In Boston

46   The next day, Archer arrived in a hot sunny Boston. He sent a message to the Parker House, where Madame Olenska was staying, and when he did not get a reply, he decided to go for a walk in Boston Common, a large park in the center of the city. He started walking across the park, when he saw her sitting on the first bench under a tree.

He walked over to her, and Ellen turned and looked at him.

"Oh!" she said with a surprised look on her face. And then she smiled slowly and happily.

"I'm here on business, just got here," Archer explained. "But what are you doing here?" he continued, not really knowing what he was saying.

"I'm here on business, too," she answered.

"You do your hair differently," he said, his heart beating fast.

"It's because Nastasia isn't here with me. I'm only here for two days," she replied.

"You're alone at the Parker House?" Archer asked.

"Yes. Why, do you think it's dangerous?" Ellen replied.

"No, not dangerous, but it's unconventional."

"I suppose it is. I hadn't thought of it. I've just done something much more unconventional. I've refused to take back money that belonged to me," she explained.

"Someone has come here with an offer?" he wanted to know.

Ellen nodded.

"And you refused because of the conditions?"

"I refused."

"What were the conditions?" he asked again.

"Nothing difficult, just to sit at the head of his table now and then," she explained.

There was an interval of silence. Archer's heart had slammed itself shut.

"He wants you back, at any price?" he asked nervously.

"Well, a considerable[1] price. At least it's considerable for me."

"So, you came here to meet him," Archer concluded.

"My husband? Here?" Ellen started laughing. "At this season he's always at Cowes or Baden. No, he sent someone."

"His secretary?" Archer asked carefully.

"Yes. He's still here, and he insisted[2] on waiting until this evening. In case I changed my mind," she said. Then, looking at his face, she spoke again. "You haven't changed, Newland."

He felt like answering, "I had, until I saw you again." But instead he stood up quickly and looked around. Then he started talking.

48 "Spend the day with me! I'll say anything you like, or nothing. I won't open my mouth unless you tell me to. All I want is some time with you. All I want is to listen to you. I want to get you away from that man. When is he coming to the hotel?"

"At eleven," she replied, feeling nervous.

"Then we must leave now," he said. "I only want to hear about you, to know what you've been doing. It's a hundred years since we've met, and it may be another hundred before we meet again."

She became anxious then.

"Why didn't you come down to the beach to fetch me, the day I was at Granny's?" she asked.

"Because you didn't look around, and because you didn't know I was there. I decided not to unless you looked around." He laughed as he realized how childish this was.

"But I didn't look around on purpose."

"On purpose?"

"I knew you were there; when you drove in I recognized the carriage. So I went down to the beach."

"To get away from me as far as you could?"

She repeated in a low voice: "To get away from you as far as I could."

---

1 considerable [kənˈsɪdərəbl̩] (a.) 可觀的
2 insist [ɪnˈsɪst] (v.) 堅持

After these confessions Madame Olenska and Newland walked back to the hotel to leave a note for Count Olenski's secretary. Ellen took the message inside while Archer waited for her anxiously outside.

As he was walking up and down outside, he saw a man who looked familiar, maybe foreign, who disappeared into the crowd. Then the doors opened again and she was at Archer's side once more.

They went on a boat trip. They sat in silence on the half-empty boat, enjoying their nearness. When they stopped for lunch, Ellen told Archer that she felt tired of New York society, and she had decided to try Washington where she could meet more varieties of people and opinion.

"I wonder why you don't go back to Europe," Archer exclaimed as he listened to her.

"I believe it's because of you," Ellen answered.

This confession embarrassed Archer and he could not move or speak.

"Because of me? I'm the man who married one woman because another one told him to," he answered.

"You promised not to say such things today," she replied.

"How like a woman! You never want to face anything bad."

"And is it bad for May? How does she feel? That's the thing we should think of." Ellen spoke her cousin's name with tenderness[1].

May and Ellen

- What does Ellen think of May?
- What does May think of Ellen?

50 　"You showed me real life, and then you asked me to live a false one. I can't bear[2] it anymore," said Archer.

"I can't bear it, either," replied Ellen and she started crying quietly.

In a moment, there they were: close together and safe. Yet they both knew that their destinies were separate.

"When will you go back?" Archer cried. But he really wanted to ask, "How can I keep you?"

"I won't go back yet," she replied.

"What a life for you!" Archer said.

"Oh, as long as it's a part of yours," Ellen replied.

"And mine a part of yours?" Archer asked back.

Ellen did not say a word; she just nodded. Then they sat there, only holding each other's hands from a distance.

"Don't be unhappy," she said.

"You won't go back?" he answered.

"I won't go back," she said, ending their conversation.

1　tenderness [ˈtɛndənəs] (n.) 溫柔
2　bear [bɛr] (v.) 忍受（動詞三態：bear–bore–borne）

14. Ellen's future

On his way back to New York, Archer was calm, and he felt as if a kind of golden haze[1] surrounded him. As he was leaving the train station, the gentleman he saw at the Parker House walked towards him and greeted him.

It was Monsieur Rivière, the Frenchman he and May had met in London. Suddenly Archer realized that he was the secretary that Madame Olenska's husband had sent to Boston to convince Ellen to return to Europe.

Rivière explained to Archer that when he arrived in America first, he believed that it would be best for the Countess to return to her husband. He had spoken to Ellen's family and they agreed with this idea. Archer understood that he had been excluded[2] from these discussions.

Then, to Archer's surprise, Rivière begged him not to let her go back. After their meetings in Boston he had understood that Ellen had changed. That she was an American, and for someone like her it would be impossible to go back to her husband. Then the two men shook hands and Monsieur Rivière turned and walked away.

---

1 haze [hez] (n.) 薄霧
2 exclude [ɪk'sklud] (v.) 把……排除在外

Two months later, at Mrs Archer's usual Thanksgiving dinner in November, Newland clearly saw that Countess Olenska was no longer supported by her family. Even Mrs Manson Mingott had been unable to defend[1] her decision not to return to her husband.

They had simply, as May's mother said, "let poor Ellen find her own level." They said that she had become a "Bohemian." Newland noticed that when Ellen's name was mentioned, May blushed. She was not supportive of her cousin Ellen, either. It seemed that everyone had changed their minds about her.

Archer and Madame Olenska had not spoken since the hot summer day they had spent together. He knew that she had returned to Washington, where she and her mother shared a house.

When he wrote to her asking when they could meet again, she replied with two words: "Not yet."

At the dinner people talked about Julius Beaufort's business problems and they feared that everyone would suffer financially.

Sillerton Jackson said that it was a pity Madame Olenska refused to accept her husband's offer.

"Well, to put it simply," he said, "what's she going to live on[2] now?"

"Now?" Archer asked.

"Well, I know from her grandmother that the family has reduced Countess Olenska's allowance[3] because of this refusal. Most of her money is invested with Beaufort, and now that could be lost as well."

"I'm sure she won't go back now," Archer replied.

"That might be your opinion, but she will have to survive somehow. Madame Olenska might convince her grandmother to give her money, but we know that her family does not want to keep her here in America."

When May and Newland arrived home after the Thanksgiving dinner, Archer announced that he needed to go to Washington because of work in the near future. May understood why he was suddenly interested in going there, but she did not tell Archer. She only suggested that he should go and see Ellen. Archer knew that his wife knew exactly why he wanted to go to Washington.

1　defend [dɪˋfɛnd] (v.) 為……辯護
2　live on 維生
3　allowance [əˋlaʊəns] (n.) 津貼；零用錢

15. Mrs Mingott has a stroke[1]

The following Wednesday, when Archer went to work, Mr Letterblair met him with a worried face. Beaufort was in ruins and he had ruined many other people with him. It was the biggest financial disaster in the history of Wall Street. As they were speaking, a letter arrived for Archer from May.

Old Mrs Mingott had had a stroke the night before, and May's family needed Archer there. He left immediately. May met him at the door, pale but smiling. He learnt that Regina Beaufort had visited old Mrs Mingott the night before, asking for support for her husband.

"Your name was Beaufort when he covered you with jewels, and it has to stay Beaufort now that he's covered you with shame," Mrs Mingott had said to Regina.

Mrs Beaufort left after an hour and Mrs Mingott went to bed, visibly distressed[2]. At three in the morning she rang the bell for help.

The whole family—including Archer—agreed that a wife's place was with her husband, and the tie[3] between husband and wife was stronger than her tie to her wider family.

---

1   stroke [strok] (n.) 中風
2   distressed [dɪˈstrɛst] (a.) 痛苦的
3   tie [taɪ] (n.) 關係

85

55 Fortunately, the stroke was not serious and soon Mrs Mingott was able to give orders once more. She asked her maid to send a telegram to Ellen Olenska, asking her to visit her grandmother. Archer sent the telegram, and offered to collect[1] Ellen at Jersey train station.

May was surprised to hear that Newland did not have to go to Washington any longer. He knew she realized that he had told a lie, and he felt bad when she pretended not to understand.

As he was leaving, all he could think was that he would have two hours to spend with Ellen during the journey from Jersey to Mrs Mingott's place.

Archer walked up and down waiting for Ellen in Jersey City Station on a dark snowy afternoon. He imagined her getting off the train and him seeing her in the distance. It was incredible[2] the number of things he had to say to her.

Waiting

- How does Archer feel as he waits for Ellen's train? Tick (✓):
  ☐ nervous ☐ excited ☐ happy
  ☐ upset ☐ confused
- Have you ever felt like this while you were waiting for someone?

"This way, I have the carriage," he said as he drew her arm through his.

"How is Granny?" Ellen asked softly.

"She's much better; she's all right, really," said Archer holding Ellen's hand.

Then he took off her tight brown glove and kissed her palm.

"You didn't expect me today?" he asked.

"Oh, no," she replied.

"I hardly remembered you. But you know, it's always like this, each time you happen to me all over again," Archer said.

"Oh, yes, I know, I know!" Ellen replied and confessed the same feelings.

As they were sitting next to each other, they discussed Monsieur Rivière's visit and how he was helping Ellen to get away from her husband. Ellen's honesty amazed Archer. She thought that the events in her life made her stronger.

"My tears have dried up," she said to Archer.

"You must see that this thing between us can't last," Archer said to her.

"What can't?" Ellen wanted to know.

"Our being together—and not together."

"You should not be here today," Ellen said, then suddenly she kissed him.

---

1 collect [kəˈlɛkt] (v.) 接走
2 incredible [ɪnˈkrɛdəbl̩] (a.) 難以置信的

"You are so much more than I remembered, and I want more than an hour or two every now and then with you. I can be patient next to you, and quietly trust it to come true," Archer said.

"Is it your idea that I should live with you even if I can't be your wife?" Ellen asked him.

"I want somehow to get away with you into a world where we can be simply two human beings who love each other, who are the whole of life to each other."

"Oh, my dear, where is that country?" Ellen sighed and laughed at him.

"Then what is your plan for us?" he asked.

"For us? There is no us. We do not have a future," Ellen replied.

Archer sat silent, dazed[1] with a sharp pain. Then he stopped the carriage and left Ellen on her own saying, "You're right. I should not have come today."

He started crying and felt the tears freezing on his eyelashes.

16. Alone in New York

(58) Newland and May were sitting in the library of their home that evening. Archer was reading a book about history, and May was doing embroidery². Archer was struck³ by the deadly monotony⁴ of their lives. May would never surprise him with an unexpected mood or idea. He stopped reading and stood up impatiently.

"What's the matter?"

"It's hot in here. I want a little air," and he opened a window and leaned out into the dark icy winter evening.

"Newland, shut the window. You'll be sick," May shouted at him.

Then he thought to himself, "I've been dead for months and months."

One day, Mrs Manson Mingott asked to see him. He hoped that he would have the chance to see Ellen. When he went over to Mrs Mingott's, he realized that Ellen was out, and old Mrs Mingott wanted to speak to him alone.

1 daze [dez] (v.) 使眩惑；使昏迷
2 embroidery [ɪmˋbrɔɪdərɪ] (n.) 刺繡
3 strike [straɪk] (v.) 打擊
  （動詞三態：strike–struck–struck, stricken）
4 monotony [məˋnɑtənɪ] (n.) 單調；千篇一律

"Well, it's decided! Ellen's going to stay with me, whatever the family say!" she said immediately.

Archer listened in silence. He had thought that they might be able to travel and live happily, far away, maybe in Japan. He was stunned[1] when he left and walked towards the Beaufort house hoping to find Ellen there.

"Ellen, I will see you now and we will be together," he said abruptly when he saw her in the street.

"Ah," she answered, "Granny has told you?"

"Tomorrow I must see you—somewhere where we can be alone," said Archer.

"Alone in New York?" Ellen asked.

"There's the Art Museum in the Park. Meet me there at half past two. I will be at the door."

She turned away and got quickly into her carriage, and he thought that she waved her hand.

"She will come!" he said to himself.

"I believe you came to New York because you were afraid," Archer said to her at the museum the next day.

"Afraid?" Ellen asked.

"Of me visiting you in Washington."

"Well, yes," she said.

"Well, then?" he asked

"Well, then; this is better, isn't it?" she sighed.

"No. I told you what I want," Archer said.

"I promised I would stay with Granny because I think I shall be safer there."

"From me? Safer from loving me?" Archer asked.

"I can't stay with her and lie to my family," Ellen replied.

"That's why I ask you to come away with me!" Archer said.

"I must go," Ellen said.

"Let's meet again tomorrow," Archer asked her.

"The day after," she replied after some time.

"My dear!" he said.

"Oh, I'll be late. Goodbye."

She walked away in a hurry, turning back for a moment to wave at him when she reached the door.

When Archer arrived home he was surprised to see that May was still out. He entered the library and sat down in his armchair.

He was sitting there in silence when the door opened and May came in.

"I'm very late. You weren't worried, were you?" she asked.

Archer looked confused. "Is it late?"

---

1   stunned [stʌnd] (a.) 錯愕的

"After seven. I went to see Granny, and I was just leaving when Ellen arrived from a walk, so I stayed and had a long talk with her. It's been ages since we've had a real talk. She was so nice, just like the old Ellen. I'm afraid I haven't been fair to her lately. She is different from other people, but I don't want to judge her."

Archer realized how much May really hated Ellen and how much she was trying to deal with this feeling.

Feelings

- How does May feel?
- How does Archer feel?
- Are they being truthful to each other?
- Why? Why not?

17. The farewell dinner

The van der Luydens were back in New York to support all the families who had been shaken by the Beaufort crisis.

One evening they invited May and Newland to go with them to the opera. May wore her bridal dress as it was the custom for brides to wear their wedding dress during the first year or two of their marriage. So just like the night two years ago, May was in white and Faust was on stage. As they were listening to the music, Archer suddenly wanted to leave the place, and asked May to go with him.

When they arrived home, Archer felt he needed to talk to May about his feelings.

"Madame Olenska . . ." he started when May interrupted him.

"It doesn't matter now, when it's all over," she said.

Archer looked at her blankly[1]. "All over—what do you mean?"

"She is going back to Europe very soon. Granny accepted her decision, and she has given her enough money to make her independent."

It was hard for Archer to control himself.

---

1 blankly ['blæŋklɪ] (adv.) 茫然地

"It's impossible," he exclaimed. "How do you know this?"

"I saw Ellen yesterday, I told you. I saw her at Granny's."

"Did she tell you yesterday?"

"No, I received a note from her this afternoon."

Then she went up to Archer and pressed his cold hand against her cheek.

It was May's idea to give their first big dinner as a young couple to say farewell to Ellen. Even the van der Luydens stayed in New York for the occasion.

Everything was arranged perfectly: the menu cards, the lamps, the tables, the flowers, the silver baskets and the candles. The most important members of the family and their friends were invited, and Ellen enjoyed special attention all through the meal.

Archer was sitting next to Ellen. He suddenly realized that the whole family had been watching him for a long time, that they thought that Ellen and he were lovers. He felt like a prisoner in the center of an armed camp.

He turned to Ellen and started chatting about train journeys in America and Europe. Then the table discussed trips to Italy, and agreed that India was interesting to visit.

Watching

- Who is watching Archer?
- What are they thinking?

Archer saw Ellen for the last time in their hallway as she was leaving. He wanted to walk her to the carriage, but Mr van der Luyden said they were driving her home.

"Goodbye," Ellen said.

"Goodbye. I will see you soon in Paris," he answered.

"Oh, if you and May could come . . ." she said.

He saw her face once more and she was gone.

Later, in the library May wanted to discuss the evening with Newland.

"It was beautiful. Can I come and talk it over?" she asked.

"Of course, but aren't you sleepy?" Archer answered.

"No, I'm not sleepy, and I would like to sit with you."

"Very well," he answered.

"I tried to tell you something the other night," Archer continued. "I am horribly tired, and I want to go on holiday."

"Oh I have seen it, Newland! You have worked so much lately!" May replied anxiously.

"I want to go on a long trip, away from everything," he said. "Maybe to India."

"That far? I'm afraid you can't, dear. My doctors won't let me go with you. Newland, I have been sure since this morning of something I've hoped for. I'm expecting a baby."

"Oh, my dear," he said, holding her to him.

There was silence between them.

"You did not guess?" May asked.

"Have you told anyone else?" Archer asked.

"Only my mother. And Ellen. You know I told you we'd had a long talk one afternoon."

"Ah!" cried Archer, his heart stopping.

"Do you mind me telling her first, Newland?" May asked.

"Why should I?" he replied, trying to stay calm. "But that was two weeks ago. I thought you said you weren't sure until this morning."

She blushed and looked at him. "No, I wasn't sure then, but I told Ellen I was. And you see, I was right!" she answered with victory in her blue eyes.

18. In Paris

Newland Archer was sitting in the room where most of the real things of his life had happened. There, his first child, Dallas, had been christened, his second child, Mary, had announced her engagement to a boring but reliable man, and he and May had discussed the studies of their sons, Dallas and Bill.

Newland had always been a good citizen, a respected lawyer, whose opinion mattered to the public. He was a loving father and a faithful husband.

When May died of pneumonia[1], he honestly mourned[2] her. He still had his first photograph of May on his writing table. All through her life, she had no imagination and was unable to notice change. This made her children and Archer hide their views from her. She died thinking the world a good place, full of loving families like her own.

As Archer sat thinking, the telephone rang. His son Dallas was calling from Chicago to tell him that a client wanted him to look at some gardens in Italy. He was inviting his father on a last trip to Europe as father and son before he got married to Fanny Beaufort, the beautiful daughter of Julius Beaufort, from his second marriage.

---

1   pneumonia [njuˈmonjə] (n.) 肺炎
2   mourn [morn] (v.) 哀悼

Paris filled Archer's heart with the confusion and happiness of youth. He had not visited the city since he was a young man, and he knew that he might meet Madame Olenska. Archer thought that he had everything, except one thing, the flower of life.

When he thought of Ellen, he thought of her as an imaginary person in a book he loved. She became the symbol of the things he had missed. And now he had the chance to meet her again.

(68) "I've got a message for you. Countess Olenska expects us both at half past five," Dallas said to his father on the day after they arrived in Paris.

Archer looked at him.

"Fanny made me promise to do three things while I was in Paris. Get her the score of the last Debussy songs, go to the Grand-Guignol and see Madame Olenska. You know she was good to Fanny, and she is also our cousin."

Archer continued to stare at his son. "Did you tell her I was here?"

"Of course, why not? She sounds lovely. What was she like?" Dallas answered.

"Lovely? I don't know. She was different."

"Well, she was the woman you wanted to throw away everything for? But you didn't."

"I didn't," said Archer solemnly[1].

"Mother said the day before she died that we were safe with you, because once, when she asked you to, you had given up the thing you most wanted."

Archer looked at his son in silence, and then he said in a low voice: "She never asked me."

"No. I forgot. You never asked each other anything. You never told each other anything. You just sat and watched each other and guessed what was going on underneath," his son replied.

---

1 solemnly [ˈsɑləmlɪ] (adv.) 嚴肅地

69 In the afternoon Dallas went to Versailles and Archer went to the Louvre. Ellen had told him that she often went there.

Father and son met back at the hotel and together they walked towards Ellen's house. Suddenly he whispered to himself, "But I'm only fifty-seven."

He knew it was too late for a new summer love, but surely it was not for a quiet autumn friendship. More than thirty years divided them, and he knew very little about her life since he had last seen her.

The sun was shining softly when Archer and Dallas arrived at Ellen's house. It was a modern building and had lots of windows and balconies on its cream-colored front. On one of the windows the awnings[1] were still open to let the last of the evening sunlight in.

"The porter says it's on the fourth floor," Dallas said to his father.

They both looked up at the window without the awning.

"That must be it," said Dallas.

Then Archer saw an empty bench under a tree.

"I'll sit there for a moment," he said to Dallas.

"Why, aren't you well?" Dallas asked.

"Oh, perfectly. But I would like you, please, to go up without me."

"Do you mean that you won't come, Dad?"

---

1 awning [ˈɔnɪŋ] (n.) 涼篷；雨篷

"I don't know," said Archer slowly.

"She won't understand," Dallas replied.

"Go, my son. Maybe I'll follow you."

"But what will I tell her?" Dallas asked.

"You always know what to say," Archer said with a smile.

"I'll tell her you're old-fashioned and prefer walking up instead of taking the elevator[1]."

"Say I'm old-fashioned; that's enough," Archer replied.

Archer sat down and continued to look at the window of her apartment. He imagined Dallas entering the room and smiling. He imagined Ellen standing up and holding out a long thin hand with three rings on it.

"It's more real to me here than if I went up," he suddenly said to himself.

He sat for a long time on the bench with his eyes on the balcony. A light shone through the windows, and a servant closed the curtains. Newland thought it was the signal he was waiting for. He got up slowly and walked back alone to his hotel.

1   elevator [ˈɛləˌvetɚ] (n.) 〔美〕電梯

AFTER READING

1 Talk About the Story

1 Answer the questions.

a What did you like or dislike about this story?

b Did you have a favorite character?
Why did you like him/her?

c Which character did you most empathize with? Why?

2 Read the quote from the story then discuss it.

> Many cruel things have been believed of me.

a Who said this?

b What do you think the cruel things are?

c Do you agree with them?

3 Discuss these questions in pairs or small groups.

a What did you learn about New York society from the story? How does it compare to the society you live in?

b Why do you think May told Ellen that she was pregnant? What does this tell us about May's character?

c Why do you think Newland decides not to visit Ellen in Paris?

2 Comprehension

1 Tick (✓) T (true) or F (false).

T F (a) Newland Archer wanted to arrive early at the opera.

T F (b) Mrs Mingott was in favor of a short engagement.

T F (c) Countess Olenska had a happy marriage.

T F (d) Mr Beaufort was a respected man.

T F (e) Newland Archer wanted to run away with Countess Olenska.

T F (f) May and Newland both enjoyed their long European honeymoon.

T F (g) May and Newland had four children.

T F (h) Newland decided to meet Ellen in Paris.

2 Correct the false sentences in Exercise **1**.

3 What do you remember from the beginning of the story? Ask and answer with a friend.

(a) Where did Newland see Ellen for the first time?

(b) Why was Newland nervous about going to the Beauforts' ball?

(c) What is the relationship between May and Countess Olenska?

(d) What was the gossip about Countess Olenska?

(e) Who was the first person Newland and May visited after their engagement?

(f) What did we learn about the Beauforts?

4 Put these scenes from the story in chronological order (1-3).

5 Write a couple of sentences to describe each scene in Exercise **4**. Include the place, the people and what is happening.

6 Read the sentences from the story and discuss them with a partner. Then, find two more examples of conventions in New York high society in the story.

> He was not worried about his late arrival.
> It was not "the thing" to arrive early at the opera.

> It always happened the same way. After the first night of the opera there was a ball at the Beauforts.

> "You're alone at the Parker House?" Archer asked.
> "Yes. Why, do you think it's dangerous?" Ellen replied.
> "No, not dangerous, but it's unconventional."

7 With a partner make a list of conventions in your society today.

3 **Characters**

1 Complete the sentences with the words in the box.

> aristocracy   dared   different   interesting
>
> reasonable   secrets   shy   superior

a) Newland Archer thought of himself as _____ to the other men in the New York upper class.

b) Countess Olenska was _____ from the rest of New York society.

c) She was beautiful and popular and the most _____ of wives.

d) Old Mrs Mingott, the head of the family, _____ to do anything she wanted.

e) Julius Beaufort was a hospitable Englishman with mysterious _____ .

f) Mrs Archer and her daughter Janey were both _____ women.

g) The van der Luydens were one of the three families that made up the _____ of New York.

h) In London, Archer had an _____ talk with Monsieur Rivière, a French tutor.

2 Discuss the van der Luydens in pairs or small groups.

a) Why are they important to New York high society?

b) How do they affect the lives of the three main characters: Ellen, May and Newland?

c) How are the van der Luydens different to the other characters in the story?

3 Compare Ellen and May. Write the words under their names and then talk about each character.

> sporty   likes art   different
> conventional   yellow roses   lilies-of-the-valley
> innocent   mysterious   popular
> black sheep of the family

Ellen

May

4 Who says these things? Match the sentences to the characters.

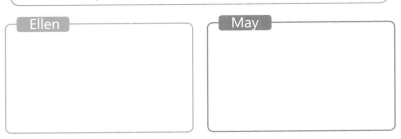

Newland Archer   Ellen Olenska   Mrs Mingott   Mr van der Luyden

- [a] It is the principle that I dislike.
- [b] Each time you happen to me all over again.
- [c] The real loneliness is living among all these kind people who only want you to pretend.
- [d] Know each other? Nonsense! Everybody in New York has always known everybody.

5 Put the quotations in context. When were these things said? To whom?

4 Vocabulary

1 In the story people don't always say how they are feeling, but their body language helps us to understand. Look at the words in the box and find examples of how they are used in the story. Then act out their meanings with a partner.

> gaze   glance   nod   redden
> sigh   stare   tremble

2 Complete the sentences from the story with words from Exercise **1**. Write them in the correct forms.

a Neither Archer, nor Ellen moved, and for a long moment he stood on the bank, _____ at the sea.

b Newland Archer _____ and laughed.

c Ellen did not say a word; she just _____.

d Archer started _____ and checking his diary.

e She _____ at him understandingly.

f Archer continued to _____ at his son.

g "Well, then; this is better, isn't it?" she _____.

3 Match the words and the definitions.

_____	a admire	1	love someone very much
_____	b adore	2	respect someone very much
_____	c consent	3	hate someone and have no respect for them
_____	d despise	4	give approval; agree to do something
_____	e persuade	5	make someone agree with you
_____	f pretend	6	behave in a way to make someone believe that something is true when it is not

4 Complete the sentences with the words from Exercise **3**. You might have to change the verb form.

a. Mrs Mingott _____ the diamond arrow that May had won.

b. "Oh, it's a poor little place. My family _____ it."

c. Parents _____ wedding. Tuesday after Easter.

d. Mother and daughter _____ each other and respected their son and brother.

e. The next day he _____ May to go for a walk in the park after lunch.

f. "The real loneliness is living among all these kind people who only want you to _____!"

5 Match the two halves to make sentences.

_____ a. It was obvious that old Mrs Mingott, the head of the family,

_____ b. She was surrounded by a group of happily laughing friends,

_____ c. He felt disappointed to learn that Madame Olenska was away,

_____ d. The old lady was grateful to him

_____ e. "You announced your engagement at the Beaufort ball

_____ f. She was simple and nice to everyone,

1. who were all delighted to hear about her engagement.

2. for persuading Countess Olenska to give up the idea of a divorce.

3. and then immediately remembered that he had an invitation to spend the weekend with some friends.

4. so there would be two families to stand by me."

5. and no one could ever be jealous of her.

6. dared to do anything she wanted.

5 **Language**

1 Connect these words to make meaningful expressions you have read in the text. Do you remember who they are used to describe?

_____ ⓐ shameful   ① beauty
_____ ⓑ luxurious   ② figure
_____ ⓒ mysterious   ③ past
_____ ⓓ simple   ④ lifestyle
_____ ⓔ slight   ⑤ behavior

2 Discuss the meanings of these phrasal verbs from the text.

ⓐ to run away with   ⓓ to get away
ⓑ to take after   ⓔ to set off
ⓒ to give up   ⓕ to end up

3 Use the phrasal verbs from Exercise **2** to complete these sentences. You might have to change the verb forms.

ⓐ Countess Olenska _____ her husband's secretary.

ⓑ "Not one of my children _____ me, but my little Ellen."

ⓒ The old lady was grateful to him for persuading Countess Olenska _____ the idea of a divorce.

ⓓ "She thinks that I want to marry her _____ from someone that I love more."

ⓔ The Newland Archers _____ on a three-month honeymoon to Europe.

ⓕ They all _____ laughing together at the embarrassment.

4 Read the extract from the story and answer the questions in pairs or small groups.

> "Three whole days at cold Skuytercliff!" Beaufort was talking in his loud voice as Archer entered.
>
> They were discussing Madame Olenska's visit to the van der Luyden country house.
>
> "Why? Is the house so cold?" she asked.
>
> "No, but the missus is. You should stay here and come with me to Delmonico's next Sunday and meet artists and other happy people."

(a) What does the word "missus" tell us about Mr Beaufort?

(b) What else do we learn about him in this extract?

(c) How is he different from the other people in New York's high society?

5 Change the sentences from either reported speech into direct speech or from direct speech to reported speech.

(a) She thinks it is a bad sign that I am impatient.

_____

(b) "Newland, has anything happened?"
May asked _____

(c) They also said that the Countess Olenska lived alone in Venice.

_____

(d) "My dress isn't smart enough."
She said _____

6 Plot and Theme

1 Put these events from the story into the correct order.

_____ [a] Newland tells Ellen he would love to marry her.

_____ [b] May Welland and Newland Archer announce their engagement.

_____ [c] Newland Archer sees Ellen Olenska at the opera.

_____ [d] Newland follows Ellen to Skuytercliff.

_____ [e] Newland travels to St. Augustine to convince May of an early marriage.

_____ [f] Newland Archer convinces Ellen not to divorce her husband.

_____ [g] Ellen and Newland spend a day together in Boston.

_____ [h] May and Newland get married.

2 What happens at these places? Discuss with a partner.

[a] at the opera

[b] at the ball

[c] in Skuytercliff

[d] in Boston

[e] in Switzerland, Paris and London

[f] at the pier near Newport

[g] in St. Augustine, Florida

[h] in Paris

3 New York society is described in the story both as a pyramid and a labyrinth. Draw pictures of these two structures and demonstrate how they symbolize New York and its society in the 1870s.

4 Look at the concepts below. What do they mean? Do they exist in your culture today? Discuss with a partner.

- a arranged marriage
- b engagement announcement
- c short engagement
- d long engagement
- e divorce as a scandal

5 Countess Olenska is often described as "different" or a "black sheep." With a partner make a list of examples in her life and lifestyle which make her seem different to others. Would she seem "different" today?

_____

_____

_____

_____

_____

_____

6 Read pages 71 and 104 again and answer the questions with a partner.

a What is similar about these two scenes?

b Why do you think Newland makes the decisions he does at these two moments?

c What do you think would have happened if he had made a different decision at these two moments?

d Would you have made different decisions? Why?

7 Listen to the extract from the story and discuss it in small groups. Thirty years later, has Newland Archer changed? If so, how? Is his life how he imagined it would be at the beginning of the story?

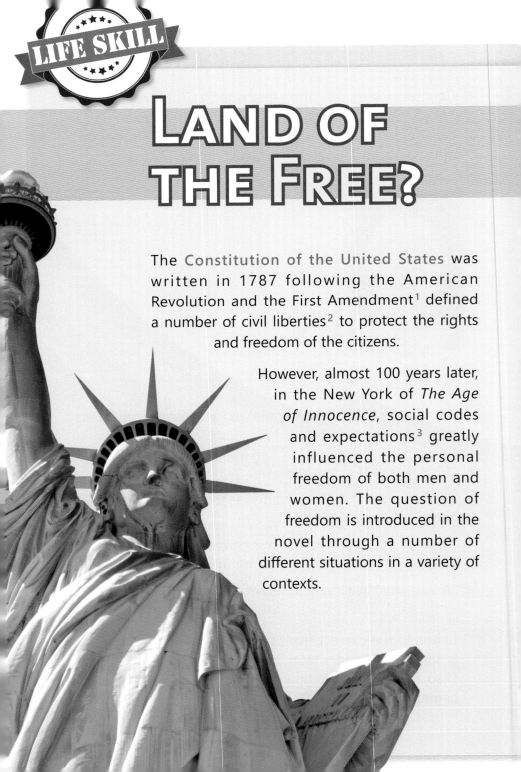

LAND OF THE FREE?

The **Constitution of the United States** was written in 1787 following the American Revolution and the First Amendment[1] defined a number of civil liberties[2] to protect the rights and freedom of the citizens.

However, almost 100 years later, in the New York of *The Age of Innocence*, social codes and expectations[3] greatly influenced the personal freedom of both men and women. The question of freedom is introduced in the novel through a number of different situations in a variety of contexts.

Civil liberties defined by the First Amendment to the US Constitution include freedom of speech, freedom of the press, freedom of religion, right to assemble[4] and right to petition. Which other freedoms and rights have been added to the Constitution?

For example, Ellen Olenska cannot simply divorce her husband and live on her own in the area of New York that she chooses. The opinions of her family and other influential families are more important than her own wishes. She depends on her family financially, and she cannot have a job like the men around her to support herself.

Although Newland Archer is a powerful man from a respected family, he is also limited in his personal freedom. He is expected to marry someone who his family approves of, whether he loves her or not.

The characters' personal freedom is somewhat limited in their everyday lives and they are expected to follow unsaid rules that dictate where and when to go out, how to dress or who to speak to. Women in particular are more limited in their choices.

1 First Amendment 美國憲法第一修正案（1791 年通過）
2 civil liberties 公民自由（通常指公民的政治自由）
3 expectation [ˌɛkspɛkˈteʃən] (n.) 期待；預期
4 right to assemble 集會自由

PERSONAL FREEDOM TODAY

A lot has changed since the nineteenth century, but change and development do not occur at the same rate in every social class, cultural context or country. Personal freedom is protected by law in most countries. However, not everyone feels that they possess the civil liberties necessary to make them free individuals. Sometimes this is due to religious conflicts, and in other cases political decisions.

The age of the internet has shown old problems of personal freedom in new contexts. Freedom of speech, privacy issues and data protection are hot issues today. The spread of social media has raised new questions in personal freedom. How can you ensure that your identity is protected? How is freedom of speech affected by social media?

From a different perspective, personal freedom is also an individual, psychological question. Can we really be free of the expectations of others and the codes of our own society? What does personal freedom mean to you?

Magna Carta
(1215)

Magna Carta is Medieval Latin for "The Great Charter[1]" and is the first legal document defining civil rights and liberties in England.

Today most clauses[2] from the Magna Carta have been rewritten or repealed[3], but a few original principles[4] remain in key[5] constitutional documents around the world, including: the United States Bill of Rights (1791), the English Bill of Rights (1689), the United Nations Universal Declaration of Human Rights (1948) and the European Convention on Human Rights (1950).

---

1 charter ['tʃɑrtə] (n.) 憲章
2 clauses [klɔz] (n.) 條款
3 repeal [rɪ'pil] (v.) 廢除（法令等）
4 principle ['prɪnsəpl] (n.) 原則
5 key [ki] (a.) 重要的

EXAM CAMBRIDGE ENGLISH EXAMS

 Bl Preliminary English Test Reading Part 5

1 Read the text below and choose the best word for each space.

He planned to go over to the Blenkers on the day of the party, when there was nobody at home. He would say he was (1) _____ in buying a horse from a farm close by. When the day came it was perfect. He arrived and stood by the gate , happy to take (2) _____ the scene. Then he walked towards the garden. There was something (3) _____ colored in the summer house. It looked (4) _____ a pink parasol, and it drew him like a magnet. He was sure that it was Ellen's. He picked it up and lifted it close to his face to (5) _____ it. He heard someone behind him and waited for Ellen's voice and touch. But it was one of the Blenker girls! She was friendly but also (6) _____ to find Archer in the garden.

1	a curious	b interested	c determined	d excited
2	a up	b off	c in	d out
3	a deeply	b lightly	c warmly	d brightly
4	a like	b as	c similar	d than
5	a smell	b taste	c touch	d hold
6	a afraid	b surprised	c scared	d worried

Bl Preliminary English Test Reading Part 6

2 Read the texts and write one word for each gap.

a The New York of that time was a small pyramid of different types of people. At the bottom were the plain respectable families. Then there were families (1) _____ the Mingotts and the Newlands. Most people imagined (2) _____ to be at the top of the pyramid, but they knew they were not. Just three families made up the aristocracy of New York, and the van der Luydens, (3) _____ were related to the Archers, (4) _____ one of them.

b Two weeks later, Newland Archer was summoned by Mr Letterblair, the head of the law firm (1) _____ he worked. He learnt (2) _____ Countess Olenska wished to get divorced (3) _____ her husband. This worried the whole Mingott family, and they sought professional advice in (4) _____ to stop the divorce from happening. Archer didn't agree (5) _____ the idea of divorce and he felt annoyed that he was being asked to deal with the case. However, when he heard that both the Mingotts and the Wellands wanted him, he reluctantly accepted the task.

TEST

72 **1** Listen and tick (√) the correct picture.

a

 1    2

b

 1    2

c

 1    2

d

 1    2

P **2** Choose the correct answer 1, 2, 3 or 4.

_____ a Ellen Olenska is May's _____
1 sister   2 friend   3 aunt   4 cousin

_____ b Why do May Welland and Newland Archer announce their engagement early?
1 They are impatient.
2 To support Ellen Olenska.
3 They want a short engagement.
4 Mrs Mingott asked them to do it.

_____ c What does Newland Archer do?
1 He is a lawyer.   2 He is a businessman.
3 He doesn't work.   4 He is a journalist.

_____ d What kind of flowers does May Welland like?
1 yellow roses   2 lilacs
3 tulips   4 lilies-of the-valley

_____ e Who supports Ellen Olenska after New York society refuses to go to the dinner in her honor?
1 Count Olenski   2 Mr Letterblair
3 the van der Luydens   4 the Duke of St. Austrey

_____ f Which sport is May good at?
1 swimming   2 tennis   3 archery   4 cricket

_____ g Who has serious business problems?
1 Sillerton Jackson   2 Julius Beaufort
3 Countess Olenska   4 Monsieur Rivière

_____ h Who is the first to know that May is pregnant?
1 Regina Beaufort   2 Ellen
3 Newland   4 Mrs Mingott

Personal freedom

In groups, choose one of the topics below.
Discuss your ideas and present them to the class.

Lifestyle and freedom

The characters of the novel cannot always choose where they want to live. Their families and their social class also influence and judge them for their professional choices, circle of friends, choice of clothes and even their personal thoughts and ideas.

- Who influences your lifestyle?
- At what age can you choose where you want to live?
- How much influence does your family have on your lifestyle?
- How much do your friends influence the way you live?
- Think about the way you dress, speak and live your everyday life. Who or what influences what you think about culture, traditions and history?

Love and freedom

Love and marriage are social institutions for the society of the novel.

- How much has society changed since the 1870s?
- Can you love and marry anyone you want to?
- Are there countries or societies today, where the family decides who someone can marry?
- How would you feel if you had to keep your love a secret?

作者簡介

P. 4–5

伊迪絲‧華頓於 1862 年一月出生於紐約一個富裕家庭，原名伊迪絲‧紐柏德‧瓊斯。家人常在歐洲旅行，伊迪絲的童年有六年在義大利、法國和德國度過。

她學過法文和德文，家人於 1872 年返回紐約後，她便在家中接受家庭教師指導。伊迪絲很幸運能使用父親的圖書館。她大量閱讀與學習，第一本詩集在 1876 年私下印行。

十七歲時，她初入社交圈，讓她可以參加在紐波特和紐約的派對和舞會。她在小說中批評這個圈子的習俗儀式。1885 年，她與愛德華（泰迪）‧華頓結婚，丈夫和她一樣喜歡旅行。

她逐漸展現對設計與園藝的熱愛，設計了她後來住了十年的房子「山峰」。她繼續和丈夫或包括作家亨利‧詹姆斯在內等友人在歐洲旅遊，她也和記者莫頓‧傅勒頓長期有染。她在 1912 年賣掉「山峰」，接著和丈夫離婚搬到巴黎。

第一次世界大戰爆發後，她透過建立女性的工作場所、難民旅舍和新醫院，對戰事有所貢獻。她也發表和戰爭有關的文章，她的表現獲頒法國榮譽軍團勳章。

戰後，她住在法國南部一個村莊，從事寫作。1921 年，她以《純真年代》獲得普立茲獎，成為第一位得到這個獎項的女性。

她於 1937 年 8 月 11 日去世，長眠於凡爾賽，與她的長期摯友華特‧貝瑞為鄰。

本書簡介

P. 6–7

　　華頓的《純真年代》是在第一次世界大戰結束之後，寫於法國。她當時已是知名作家，出版過一些小說和短篇小説。書名涉及美國歷史上的一個時期，這個年代隨著 1914 年的戰爭而結束。

　　她確實在書中回顧她於 1870 年代的紐約上層社會所度過的童年和青少年時期，並講到了當時的舞會、舞蹈和嚴格死板的規矩。美國的 1870 年代也稱為鍍金年代，在這個時代，銀行家和投資者變得有影響力，紐約市開始快速成長。當時，社會由有權有勢的家族掌控，他們有牢固的傳統和嚴格的不成文慣例。

　　小説描述梅‧韋蘭德和紐藍‧亞契的訂婚與婚姻，以及新娘的表姐艾倫‧歐蘭斯卡從歐洲來美國的故事。艾倫的出現帶來一連串的混亂，並對這對伴侶的婚姻造成威脅。

　　華頓帶著諷刺回顧這個年代，但並不批評角色的存心和行為。除了對上流階級社會運作方式的批評外，書中也因為第一次世界大戰爆發所失去的純真，而瀰漫著一股哀傷。華頓自身的生命經驗，從早期的回憶到失敗的婚姻，也都反映在小說中。

　　這本小說在 1921 年贏得普立茲獎，並啟發了好幾部改編電影的創作，包括 1993 年由馬丁‧史柯西斯執導，丹尼爾‧戴－路易斯、薇諾娜‧瑞德和蜜雪兒‧菲佛主演的知名版本。

真實世界 1870 年代的紐約社會

P. 8–9

1870 年代的紐約社會是個非常有組織的系統,它的結構就像金字塔,頂端是最有影響力和權勢的家族,下面一層是時髦的上流社會精英,新來的移民則位於底層。

原有的古老家族對新來者感到恐懼,新來者有新的價值觀和習慣,對他們的權威構成威脅。新家族通常會有不一樣的生活規則,或者是暴發戶,就像小說裡的波福特家。

四百人

當時,據估有四百人屬於紐約家族的最上層。這個說法來自艾斯特家族的大舞廳,那裡大到足以容納四百位賓客。這些家族,例如艾斯特、洛克斐勒和范德堡,他們也稱為紐約的上流社會。他們若不是因為有英國、荷蘭或法國傳統遺產,就是拜他們在生意上日漸成長的投資所賜,而成為有權有勢的家族。

他們的財富隨處顯露可見,在每個社交場合,例如婚禮、晚宴和舞會上,都可見枝型大吊燈、銀製餐具和藝術品,女性穿著綢緞、絲絨、羽毛製的奢華禮服,配戴昂貴的珠寶。

P. 10–11

規範

在小說裡,家族的風俗和傳統被形容為「儀式」,而這些家族則是「部族」。如果有人違反了社會規則,就會受到懲罰。這些規則或規範控制著眾人生活的每個層面,從每年例行活動的社會地位問題到日常行為。例如,離婚是難以接受的;舞會、歌劇之夜等等社交活動是標準的固定活動,預期每個人都要參加,而星期日出門並非潮流。

場所

紐約精英的身影可以在一些社會可接受的場所見到，例如歌劇院或私人舞廳和晚宴。舞會和晚餐顯然是較為私密的活動，而歌劇院是較為公開的場合。擁有音樂學院十八個包廂中的一個，這是重要的身分象徵。

城市裡最時髦的區域位於第三和第六大道間，而上層階級的家族大多不會搬到中央公園以北的地區。古老家族住在華盛頓廣場和鄰近區域，他們出城的目的地通常是紐波特和萊茵貝克。

社會的其他人

另外還有藝術家和作家，他們住不起城市的富裕區域。他們住在城市較為非傳統的波西米亞風格地區。貧窮的勞工階級住在結構不良、過於擁擠的公寓裡，通常是六或七個人要合住一個沒有窗戶或浴室的房間。

真實世界 鍍金年代

P. 12–15

在美國歷史上，1865 年到 1898 年間的時期通常稱為鍍金年代（Gilded Age）。那是在南北戰爭（1861–1865）之後，經濟與技術的發展達於頂峰的時期，後來隨著美西戰爭而畫下句點。

這個名稱來自馬克·吐溫和查爾斯·杜德利·華納於 1873 年所寫的《鍍金時代》一書，描述當時的政治腐敗與社會問題。書名的「鍍金」指的是表面的一層薄金掩蓋了底下的問題。

經濟力

這是經濟快速成長的時期，薪水和銀行家、實業家的個人財富都在快速增加。農業和採煤業蓬勃發展，但最成功的是新興的石油、鐵路和鋼鐵企業。

經濟力掌握在一些有錢人和他們的家族手裡，例如，約翰‧D‧洛克斐勒、安德魯‧卡內基、J. P.‧摩根和科內留斯‧范德堡。他們被稱為「強盜男爵」，因為他們是透過剝削勞工階級和操縱政局而變得有錢有勢。在這個時期，紐約的華爾街被打造為金融市場中心。

技術

這個時期也稱為第二次工業革命。沒有技術的發展和大量生產與運輸的傳入，就不會有鍍金年代。

> **強盜男爵**
>
> 你對這些家族知道些什麼？
> 他們今天以什麼聞名？
> 上網找出答案。

鋼鐵的生產變得更容易、快速，帶來鐵路的興建。太平洋鐵路（第一條橫貫大陸鐵路）於 1869 年通車，旅客只要花六天的時間，就能夠從東岸的紐約到達西岸的舊金山。大部分的鋼鐵工業都位在芝加哥附近，這個城市也在快速成長。

另一個重要的發展領域是通訊和電力。美國電話與電報公司成立於 1885 年，到今天仍在營運，AT&T 成了最大的電話公司之一。電力帶來重大的改變，街道和住家有了電力。有了人工照明，人們可以做更多工作，但也意味他們睡得更少。

大城市裡有了電車，到不同地方和其他人說話變得更容易，生意往來也變得更快速。

冷凍技術，尤其是肉類，是另一個重要的進步，這讓運送來自遠方的肉類變得更容易。

移工

大量移工從東歐、俄羅斯和義大利而來，他們住在狹小的公寓裡，在工廠裡工作。在鍍金年代，約有 1170 萬人抵達美國，這些人促成那個年代的經濟成長。他們大部分住在極為惡劣的環境裡，一天工作往往長達十二小時，他們常被稱為「建立美國」的人。

故事內文

1. 歌劇

P. 23

一八七〇年代初期，正月的一個夜晚，紐約最優雅的上流社會家族齊聚音樂學院。大夥開心地擠在藍金色相間的包廂裡，這棟狹小的建築物不是太舒服，但保守的紐約客很喜歡來這裡。

當紐藍‧亞契打開和友人共有的包廂後方的門時，歌劇早已開演。他並不擔心自己晚到，提早到歌劇院並不是「重點」。什麼是重點、什麼不是重點，這對紐藍‧亞契來說是很重要的。

在他正對面的是曼森‧明葛特老夫人的包廂。老夫人因為體型過於碩大，無法前來劇院，但是她的女兒韋蘭德夫人和媳婦洛薇兒‧明葛特夫人在裡面。和這兩位夫人坐在一起的是一個年輕女孩，她穿著白色洋裝，膝上放著一束歐鈴蘭，她是梅‧韋蘭德，是紐藍‧亞契的心上人，也是他未來的妻子。

P. 24

紐藍看著未來的妻子，想著他們會一起閱讀，他很欣賞她的純真。

他想要她變得聰明機智又迷人。如果要他說實話，他希望她像那個他相戀了兩年的已婚女子一樣有趣，當然，不要有那個女子的一絲憂傷。

歌劇

•和夥伴討論你對歌劇的認識。
•你能說出任何一齣歌劇的名字嗎？

紐藍‧亞契自認為比紐約上層階級的其他男人都要優秀，比他們任何人都讀過更多書、更常思考，也見過更多世面。然而，他不想表現得與眾不同，所以認同他們的一切道德價值觀。

當亞契站在那裡想著這些事情時，包廂裡的其他男人正在談論和梅一家人坐在一起的一位女士。亞契意識到他們在談論的是梅·韋蘭德的表姊，她剛從歐洲回來，他們稱她是「可憐的艾倫·歐蘭斯卡」。

P. 25

她是這個家族的家醜，明葛特家竟會把她帶到歌劇院這種公開場合來，這讓亞契很意外。顯然，這個家族的大家長明葛特老夫人，敢做任何她想做的事。

亞契還是不願意去想自己的未婚妻可能被撞見和一個剛離開丈夫的女人在一起，就算那個丈夫很殘暴。大家還說，歐蘭斯卡伯爵夫人和丈夫的祕書一起逃走，然後獨自住在威尼斯。

聽著這些八卦，紐藍·亞契突然想和這些女士坐在一起，好讓世人知道他和梅訂婚了，而且他力挺她的家人。

艾倫·歐蘭斯卡

- 關於艾倫·歐蘭斯卡的八卦是什麼？
- 你認為她的感受如何？

2. 訂婚

P. 26

按慣例，歌劇首演後，波福特家會舉行舞會。他們家是紐約少數有大舞廳的房子。他們的房子和生活方式都很奢華，這彌補了他們那見不得人的過去。蕾吉娜·波福特夫人來自南方一個家道中落的高尚家族，她的丈夫朱利亞斯·波福特是個英國佬，他為人親切好客，有著不為人知的祕密。他和蕾吉娜的婚姻讓他被紐約社會接受，但並未讓他因此得到別人的尊敬。

看完歌劇之後，亞契沒有和其他年輕男子一起回到他的俱樂部，而是獨自走在第五大道上，然後回頭往波福特家的方向走去。亞契很緊張，他怕明葛特家會帶歐蘭斯卡伯爵夫人去參加舞會。

亞契抵達時，梅·韋蘭德站在舞廳一側，手裡拿著歐鈴蘭花束。她被一群快樂歡笑的朋友包圍著，他們都很高興聽到她訂婚了。

P. 27

社會

- 在一八七○年代的紐約社會，財富與家族非常重要，今天還是一樣嗎？
- 如果是，為什麼？如果不是，又是為什麼？

紐藍走過去，帶著梅進入舞池。音樂結束後，他們一起走進溫室。

「你看，我照你的要求去做了。」她說。

「但不一定是要在舞會上。」

「是的，我知道。」她善解人意地瞥了他一眼，「但終究，就算是在這裡，我們也是單獨在一起，不是嗎？」

「噢，親愛的，永遠都是！」亞契大喊。

「你告訴我表姐艾倫了嗎？」她問。

「沒有，我還沒有機會，」他撒謊。

她看起來很失望，「你一定要跟她說，因為我也沒說。」

「但我還沒見到她，她有來嗎？」亞契問道。

P. 29

「沒有，她在最後一刻決定不來了。她說自己的穿著不夠時髦，不足

以去參加舞會，我舅媽只好帶她回家。」梅答道。

當然，亞契知道她表姐不來參加舞會的真正原因，但是他不想讓未婚妻知道自己清楚可憐的艾倫·歐蘭斯卡的壞名聲。

梅和紐藍

- 他們在一起快樂嗎？你為什麼這麼認為？

第二天，這對年輕人按慣例進行了首次訂婚後的拜訪。曼森·明葛特夫人是位受人敬重的老夫人，紐約大部分的家族都和她有親戚關係。她很榮幸當第一個祝福小倆口的人。

明葛特夫人住在一棟靠近中央公園的奶油色石造房子。隨著她的體重愈來愈重，她愈來愈不可能上樓或下樓，便決定睡在一樓。

P. 30

從起居室就能看得到臥室，這是很少見的，這樣的格局讓訪客感到新奇。她大部分的時間都坐在起居室的窗邊，平靜地等候生活和時尚來到她的門前。

「婚禮訂在什麼時候？」明葛特夫人問道，看著這對未婚夫妻。

「如果你贊同，愈快愈好。」亞契答道。

「應該給他們時間多熟悉彼此，媽媽。」韋蘭德夫人說。

「熟悉彼此？這是廢話嘛！在紐約，人人都熟悉彼此。就在大齋期之前結婚！我要主持婚宴。」

這次的拜訪在歐蘭斯卡伯爵夫人和朱利亞斯・波福特到來時結束。伯爵夫人看著亞契，臉上堆著笑容。

「你想必已經知道梅和我的事了。」他說。

「我當然知道，沒錯，我很高興。」她答道，伸出手來，「再見，改天要來看我。」她說道，眼睛盯著亞契看。

3. 亞契一家人

P. 32

第二天晚上，席勒頓・傑克森老先生和亞契家人共進晚餐。亞契夫人和女兒珍妮都是害羞的女性。母女倆彼此深愛著對方，也尊敬自己的兒子和兄弟，而紐藍・亞契也深愛著她們。每當亞契夫人想知道紐約重要家族生活上的任何事情時，就會邀傑克森先生共進晚餐。

這個城市的重要家族有兩種，一種是像明葛特和曼森這種家族，他們關心飲食、服飾和金錢，一種是像亞契－紐藍－馮‧德‧萊登家族，他們喜愛旅行、園藝和優異小說。

「紐藍的新表姐，歐蘭斯卡伯爵夫人呢？她也去參加舞會了嗎？」亞契夫人問道。

「沒有，她沒去。」傑克森先生答道。

「波福特家大概不認識她。」珍妮暗指。

「波福特夫人可能不認識，但是波福特先生一定認識。今天下午，有人看到他們走在第五大道上。」傑克森先生說。

「反正，不去舞會對她最好。」亞契夫人說，顯現出不認同。

「梅說她原本想去，但是覺得自己的穿著不夠時髦。」亞契發表意見。

「可憐的艾論，她和我們是那麼不同。」亞契夫人補充道。

「如果她願意，為什麼不可以與眾不同？只是婚姻失敗，不表示她就應該受到懲罰。」她的兒子生氣地回答。

「我想那是明葛特家的看法。」傑克森先生說。

年輕人的臉色都發紅了，「我不需要等待他們的看法，如果你指的是這個意思，先生。歐蘭斯卡夫人過得不快樂，但她是我們這個圈子的人。」

「我聽說她想離婚。」珍妮說。

「但願如此！」亞契大聲說。

幾天之後，發生了難以想像的事情。明葛特夫人發出正式晚宴的邀請，要大家和歐蘭斯卡伯爵夫人見面。四十八個小時之後，除了波福特家、傑克森老先生和他的姊姊，其他人都拒絕參加。

這個衝擊出乎意料之外，但明葛特家優雅以對。他們聯絡亞契家，亞契夫人決定去拜訪馮‧德‧萊登家。

當時候的紐約是個由許多不同人組成的小金字塔，底層是平凡而受人尊敬的家族，然後是像明葛特和紐藍這樣的家族。大部分人把他們想成居於金字塔頂端，但他們知道自己不是。只有三個家族組成紐約的貴族階級，而和亞契家有親威關係的馮‧德‧萊登家是其中之一。

「我們要去找他們談，是因為梅的關係，還有，我們要是不團結在一起，就沒有社會這個組織存在了。」亞契的母親說。

馮‧德‧萊登先生說：「這就是我不喜歡的行為準則，知名家族的成員只要得到家族的支持，其他人就應該接納他。」馮‧德‧萊登先生繼續說：「沒想到情況變得這麼棘手。」

137

接著，在妻子的同意下，他決定邀請歐蘭斯卡伯爵夫人參加他們為聖奧斯特里公爵和幾位特別挑選的朋友所舉行的晚宴。

P. 36

晚宴那天，歐蘭斯卡伯爵夫人很晚才抵達馮・德・萊登家，但她從容自在地走進客廳。當她在房間中間停下來時，亞契注意到她帶著神祕感的美麗和自然的舉止。她的動作和聲音很平靜，不像大家期待的那種氣派。

馮・德・萊登家盡力宣傳了這個晚上的重要性。女士們都戴著鑽石項鍊，穿著優雅的禮服，除了聖奧斯特里公爵和歐蘭斯卡伯爵夫人兩位貴賓，他們看起來沒有其他人醒目。

晚餐之後，伯爵夫人穿過客廳，坐在亞契身邊。女子選擇坐在男子身邊，並非尋常之事。

「我要你和我談談梅，她很漂亮又聰明，你很愛她嗎？」她說。

紐藍・亞契紅著臉大笑，「男人所能給的心都給了。」

「啊，那可真是一段浪漫的愛情，不是父母安排的親事。」

「你忘了嗎？在我們國家，我們不會讓別人幫我們安排婚姻。」

P. 37

「抱歉，我忘了。我不是一直這麼記得，這裡的情況不一樣。」伯爵夫人答道。

「我很難過，但你在這裡，身邊都是你的朋友，你知道。」亞契說。

「是的，我知道，所以我才回來。」

在他們談話時，馮・德・萊登先生打斷了他們。

「那麼，明天五點以後，我等你來。」伯爵夫人在亞契準備離開時說道。

「明天。」亞契聽到自己重覆這句話，雖然兩人之前並未談到要碰面。

4. 拜訪

P. 38

紐藍在五點半時抵達歐蘭斯卡伯爵夫人家，那裡是紐約一個奇特的住宅區。她的鄰居有裁縫、記者和作家。他到達的時候，伯爵夫人不在，由女僕來迎接他，並帶他去起居室裡等候。

過了一段時間，伯爵夫人在朱利亞斯·波福特陪伴下返家，波福特隨即離去。當她走進客廳，沒有顯露絲毫驚訝之色。

「你覺得我這個奇特的住處如何？」她說：「對我來說，這裡就像天堂。」

「你布置得很討人喜歡。」他答道。

「噢，這是個拙劣的小地方，我家人厭惡這裡。」艾倫答道，坐在火爐旁邊。

「我擔心你忘了時間。」亞契補充道，意指她遲到這件事。

「為什麼？你等了很久嗎？波福特先生帶我去看一些房子。他們說我得搬家，雖然我覺得這條街還不錯。」

「這裡不夠時尚。」亞契答道。

「你覺得時尚這麼重要嗎？我只想感覺被愛、有安全感，但我的家人有點氣我自己一個人住在這裡。」

P. 39

奇特的住處

• 艾倫對自己住的地方，看重的是什麼？
• 艾倫的家人看重的是什麼？
• 你對自己的居住環境，看重的是什麼？

「我想我了解你的感受。」他說：「不過你的家人還是可以給你意見，表達不同看法，指引方向。」

「紐約是這樣一個迷宮嗎？我以為都像第五大道那樣是棋盤式的道路，街道也都以號碼來命名。」

「任何事物大概都有標籤，但不是每個人都有標籤。」亞契想利用這個機會警告她小心波福特這個人。

「這裡只有兩個人讓我覺得他們好像了解我，而且會解釋事情給我聽，你和波福特先生。」艾倫回答。

「我了解，但別忘了你的老朋友們，他們也想幫你。」他親切地答道。

P. 40

艾倫嘆了口氣，「噢，我知道！但是只有在沒有聽到我的任何不好消息時，他們才會想要幫忙。這裡沒有人想要知道真相嗎，亞契先生？真正的

139

孤獨是住在這些好心人之中，而他們只想要你偽裝！」她舉手遮臉，哭了起來。

「噢，別哭，艾倫。」他說，一邊走向她。

「這裡的人也不哭嗎？」她問道。

波福特先生

• 亞契為什麼想警告艾倫小心波福特先生？

亞契離開房子，走進寒冷的冬夜。他直接走到花店，送梅一盒每天例行的歐鈴蘭，他那天早上忘了送。

當他在寫給梅的卡片時，他注意到有一束黃玫瑰，他突然打個手勢，要送那束花給歐蘭斯卡伯爵夫人。

P. 42

第二天，他說服梅吃完午餐後去公園散步。

「每天早上醒來都能聞到我房間裡的歐鈴蘭香味，真是太好了！」她說。

「昨天比較晚送去給你，我早上抽不出時間。」亞契答道。

「但你都會記得。」

「我也送了一些花給你表姐艾倫，這麼做對嗎？」

「你真好心！不過她今天午餐時沒有說，她只有提到波福特先生和馮·德·萊登先生送給她漂亮的花束。」

「噢，我想我送的花，被波福特送的花給比下去了。」亞契惱怒地說。

之後為了讓自己分神，亞契開始談起倆人的未來，還有韋蘭德夫人希望訂婚期拉長一些。亞契只希望和梅盡快結婚，但梅是個傳統的年輕女子，想要事情慢慢來。

亞契

• 亞契感覺如何？
• 他為什麼惱怒？

5. 離婚

P. 43

　　兩星期後，紐藍‧亞契工作的律師事務所老闆雷特布雷先生把他叫去。他得知歐蘭斯卡伯爵夫人想和丈夫離婚，這讓整個明葛特家族很擔憂，他們尋求專業意見，以阻止離婚。

　　亞契不贊成離婚這個想法，老闆派這個案子給他，他覺得有點煩。不過當他聽到明葛特家和韋蘭德家都指名要他時，他不情願地接下任務。

　　看過法律文件之後，紐藍‧亞契判斷，如果要了解歐蘭斯卡夫人的說法，就得去找她。於是他寫了個訊息給伯爵夫人，詢問隔天何時可以碰面。她很快地回信說，晚餐後她會一個人在家。

P. 44

　　歐蘭斯卡伯爵夫人的女僕娜塔莎來開門時，露出了神祕的笑容。朱利亞斯‧波福特正在和伯爵夫人會面，雖然亞契並未告訴艾倫希望能夠私下會面，他還是感到生氣。

　　「整整三天待在寒冷的石魁崖！」亞契進屋時，波福特正用他的大嗓門說著。

　　他們正在討論歐蘭斯卡夫人要去造訪馮‧德‧萊登的鄉間別墅一事。

　　「怎麼了？那裡很冷嗎？」她問道。

　　「不是，是女主人很冷。你應該留在這裡，下星期日和我一起去戴爾莫尼科餐廳，見見藝術家和其他開心的人。」

　　「聽起來很有趣！我來到這裡以後，只見過一位藝術家，」艾倫回答道：「我可以考慮一下，明天早上再給你捎訊息嗎？」

　　「為什麼不現在決定呢？」波福特顯得不耐煩。

　　「因為我還有事情要和亞契先生談。」

　　波福特離開，歐蘭斯卡夫人和亞契繼續在客廳談話。

　　他說：「我來這裡是要談你和雷特布雷先生的案子，我仔細看過你給他的那些文件。」

　　「噢，你看過了？你知道，我想要自由，徹底地把過去都抹掉。」她熱切地答道。

　　「我了解。」

　　「那你會幫我嗎？」

P. 45

　　「我可能要先了解一下情況。」

　　「那是一場可怕的婚姻。」艾倫回答。

　　亞契努力解釋說，就算她想恢復自由，他們家族是不樂見離婚的。離婚在美國的法律上雖然可行，但是紐約的社會並不認同，這個醜聞會傷害她的家族。

伯爵夫人很難過地接受了亞契的建議，允諾會遵從他的意思去做。

第二天晚上在劇院，亞契和歐蘭斯卡夫人再度碰面。

「你想他明天早上會送黃玫瑰花給她嗎？」艾倫問道，轉身向著亞契並指著舞台上的戀人。

亞契一陣臉紅。他拜訪過歐蘭斯卡夫人兩次，每次都送她一盒黃玫瑰，但是沒有附上卡片。她之前沒有提過這件事，所以他想她並不知道花是他送的。這個想法讓他感到雀躍。

6. 在石魁崖

P. 46

第二天早上，亞契找遍全城都買不到黃玫瑰。

他來到辦公室之後，派信差送了張便條給歐蘭斯卡夫人，詢問當天下午是否能去拜訪她。但是三天之後，她的回覆才從石魁崖送來，她和馮·德·萊登家的人一起待在那裡。

> 在看戲時見過你之後，我逃走了。這些好心的朋友收留了我。我想要不受打擾，把事情仔細想想。你說得沒錯，他們人真好。我在這裡覺得很安心。但願你和我們在一起。
>
> 真誠地，
> 艾倫

得知歐蘭斯卡夫人離開，他感到很失望，然後隨即想起奇弗塞家的一些友人邀他一起度週末，地點就在離石魁崖幾哩遠的地方。

P. 47

他在星期五傍晚抵達，星期六便做完了鄉間週末的所有例行活動。他搭了冰上滑行船，然後去農場看馬。喝過下午茶後，他和一些其他的客人在一個角落裡談天。

但在星期日的午餐之後，他便駕車去石魁崖，然而艾倫不在，他決定步行去村子裡，希望能見到她。

不久，他就看到一個穿著紅色斗篷的纖細身影，那是她！

「啊，你來了！」她說。

「我來看看你是要逃離什麼。」他笑道。

「我知道你會來！」她投以微笑。

「因為我收到了你的字條。艾倫，你為什麼不告訴我發生什麼事了？」

當他們經過馮·德·萊登家的房子時，他們注意到門是開著的。

歐蘭斯卡夫人脫下紅色斗篷，坐上其中的一張椅子。亞契斜倚著煙囪，盯著她看。

P. 48

「你現在在笑，但當你寫信給我時，你並不快樂。」他說。

「是的，不過你來了這裡，我就感覺不到不快樂了。」她答道。

有好一會兒，她都沒說話。在那個時刻，亞契想像她走到他的身後，然後用手環抱住他的脖子。當他等待這一刻發生時，他看到有人走向房子，那是朱利亞斯·波福特。

朱利亞斯·波福特

- 回想一下，朱利亞斯曾在哪些其他的場合和歐蘭斯卡夫人在一起？
- 亞契的反應如何？
- 你覺得接下來會發生什麼事？

歐蘭斯卡夫人很快走到亞契的旁邊，匆匆把手滑進他手裡。

「所以，你是要逃離他？」亞契粗魯無禮地問道。

「我不知道他在這裡。」歐蘭斯卡夫人回答。亞契接著走到前門，猛力地打開大門，迎接波福特。

「哈囉，波福特，這邊請！歐蘭斯卡夫人在等你。」他離開時一邊說道。

P. 50

無禮

- 亞契為什麼無禮？
- 他感覺如何？

回到紐約後，接下來的兩、三天很難熬。他沒有歐蘭斯卡夫人的消息。他在俱樂部看到波福特，但是兩人沒有交談。

到了第四天傍晚，他才收到她的訊息，上面說：

明天晚點過來，我要跟你解釋一下。
艾倫。

晚餐過後，他去看了戲，午夜過後才回到家。他慢慢地把訊息又看了幾次，不知道要如何回覆。

天亮後，他決定打包行李，搭船前往佛羅里達州的聖奧古斯丁，梅和家人正在那裡避寒。

7. 短暫的訂婚

P. 51

亞契沿著聖奧古斯丁的多沙大街，走向別人指給他看的韋蘭德先生的房子時，他看到梅站在一棵木蘭樹下，陽光灑落在她頭髮上，他不明白自己為什麼拖了這麼久才來。

「紐藍，發生什麼事了嗎？」梅看到未婚夫來到這裡，一臉驚訝。

「是的，我要見你。」他回答。

她喜悅的羞紅，驅走了驚訝臉龐上的冷淡。

「告訴我，你一整天都在做什麼。」他說。

「我們去游泳、駕帆船和騎馬，有時候也會去跳舞。一些從費城和巴爾的摩來的人會在客棧野餐，他們很討人喜歡。有時候我也會去打網球。」

她說這些事情讓她很忙，所以還沒有時間讀亞契上個星期寄給她的小本書籍，不過當她正用心在默背一首詩時，怎麼有辦法看書呢？

P. 53

在他停留期間，亞契一直希望說服梅早點舉行婚禮。在他離開的前一天，他又和她談。

「我們春天就會在歐洲，去塞維爾觀賞復活節儀式。」他說。

「在塞維爾過復活節？但下星期就是大齋期了！」她笑道。

「我們可以在復活節之後就結婚，然後四月底搭船，我可以在辦公室就安排好這一切。」

她對這種可能性投以微笑。

「我們為什麼要再等一年？看著我，親愛的！你難道不明白，我有多想要你成為我的妻子嗎？」亞契突然失去耐心。

「我不知道你怎麼了，是因為你不確定你對我的感情嗎？」她說。

「噢，也許，我不知道。」他生氣地回答。

「有別人嗎？我們把話說開，紐

藍。我有時候覺得你不太一樣了，尤其是從我們宣布訂婚以後。」

「天啊！真是瘋狂！」亞契不喜歡她說這種話。

「如果不是真的，那談一談又何妨，而且就算是真的，我們何不好好談一談？你可能做了錯誤的決定。」

P. 54

「如果我做了錯誤的決定，我會向你求婚嗎？」他答道。

「有人說，幾年前你有別人。有一次，在一個舞會上，我看到你和那個女子坐在陽台。她回到屋內後，表情很哀傷，我為她感到難過。」梅耐著性子說。

「你在擔心這個嗎？但願你知道真相！」

「有我不知道的真相？」

「我是指這件陳年往事的真相。」

「紐藍，如果那表示要傷害另一個人，那我不會快樂。我們不能建立那樣的生活。如果你對那個人已經許下承諾，那就不要因為我而拋棄她！」

「沒有承諾，梅。我們之間沒有別人或其他事情。」紐藍答道。

亞契回到紐約後，給明葛特老夫人發了很多訊息。老夫人很感謝他說服歐蘭斯卡伯爵夫人打消離婚的念頭。聽到他匆促南下聖奧古斯丁見梅時，她甚至更高興了些。

「你到的時候，他們是不是都很吃驚？梅的反應如何？」她問道。

「我想要她答應在四月就結婚，我們為什麼要再浪費一年？」亞契埋怨說。

「啊，這些明葛特家的人！他們都一樣，沒有一個人想與眾不同，他們都很怕不一樣。我的孩子沒有一個像我，除了我的小艾倫。既然這樣，你為什麼不娶我的小艾倫？」

P. 55

「嗯，她不是單身。」亞契笑了起來。

「現在是來不及了，她的人生已經毀了。」明葛特夫人答道。

「我無法說服你運用你對韋蘭德家的影響力嗎，明葛特夫人？我不想要漫長的訂婚。」亞契請求。

「我看得出來。」明葛特夫人回答。

明葛特老夫人

• 明葛特夫人是什麼樣的人？列出一些形容詞。回到第 23 和 25 頁找更多線索。

就在這個時候，歐蘭斯卡夫人帶著微笑走進來。

「我正在問他為什麼不娶你，我親愛的艾倫。」

歐蘭斯卡夫人看著亞契，仍然微笑著。「那他怎麼回答？」

「親愛的，我讓你自己發現！他已經南下佛羅里達州，去見過他的心上人了。」

P. 56

「是的，我知道。」艾倫答道，仍看著亞契，「我去見你的母親，問你去哪裡了。我寫了張便條，你一直沒有回覆，我擔心你生病了。當然，當你在佛羅里達州時，你就不會想到我了！」艾倫對亞契說。

亞契起身離開，艾倫送他到門口。

「我何時能夠再見到你？」他問道。

「隨時都可以，但是如果你想再看看那間小房子，就要快一點，我下星期就要搬家了。」她答道。

「明天晚上？」亞契問道。

她點頭，「明天可以，早一點來，我晚上要出門。」

便條

• 艾倫的便條上說了什麼？查看第 50 頁。

8. 再訪歐蘭斯卡伯爵夫人

P. 57

第二天，亞契聽說艾倫的伯爵丈夫給她捎了信，說她可以隨自己的意願回到他身邊。他很震驚而且痛恨這個提議，但這提醒了他，艾倫仍是伯爵的妻子。

當亞契去見她時，她穿著一襲美麗的閃亮禮服現身。她一走進起居室，就注意到一大束讓她感到不悅的花，那是丈夫送給她的。

她立刻把娜塔莎叫來，要將花送給一個鄰居，當作驚喜。

花

- 花在這個故事裡很重要，列出到目前為止，誰送過花給誰？
- 你覺得，在每個例子中，花代表什麼意思？

「你聽說了我的什麼事？」她問亞契。

「嗯，我聽說歐蘭斯卡伯爵想要你回到他的身邊，聽說有封信。」

P. 58

「說到底，這不令人意外。」她沉默了一會兒後說:「有很多關於我的刻薄的事，大家都相信。」她微微笑了一下，「而你，紐藍，你很緊張，你也有自己的問題。我知道，你認為梅的家人不贊成你們早點結婚，但當然，我認同你。在歐洲，人們不了解我們美國人的漫長訂婚。」

「是的，我南下要求梅在復活節後嫁給我，沒有理由不該在那時候結婚。」

「梅很崇拜你，很奇怪，你竟然無法說服她。」

「我們第一次開誠布公地談，她覺得我的急躁是個壞兆頭。她也認為，這表示我無法相信自己。她覺得我之所以要和她結婚，是因為我想逃離某個我更愛的人。」

「她如果那麼想，何不趕快結婚？」艾倫問道。

「她想要長一點的訂婚期，才可以給我時間……」

「給你時間好為了另一個女人而離開她？」

「如果那是我要的。」

「那『真是』高尚。」艾倫說。

「對，但那很荒謬。」亞契答道。

「為什麼荒謬？你沒有愛著另一個女人嗎？」

「不是，而是因為我不打算娶別人。」

P. 60

「這另一個女人愛你嗎？」艾倫問道。

「是有另一個女人，但不是梅以為的那一個。」

艾倫·歐蘭斯卡沒有答話，也沒有動。

一會兒後，他在她旁邊坐下，握著她的手。

「如果情勢允許的話，你是我想娶的女人。」

「你讓我們不可能在一起。」艾倫回答。

「我讓情況變得不可能？」

「你說服我放棄離婚這個念頭，以免我的家族捲入醜聞！因為我的家人就要變成你的家人了，所以我就照你的話做了。我這麼做都是為了你！」艾倫幾乎要哭了。

「至少，我愛過你。」他告白。

他靠過去，親吻了她。僅僅是碰觸她，就讓一切都變得清楚了。

她回應了他所有的親吻，但一會兒後，她離開他的懷抱。

「你改變了我的人生。」他對艾倫說。

「不，不！你和梅訂婚了，而我已經結婚。」

「沒這種事！我們不能騙別人，也

不能騙自己。都這樣子了，我怎麼能和梅結婚？」

「我希望你不會問梅那個問題。」艾倫答道

「做什麼都於事無補了。」亞契回答。

P. 61

「你已經為我做了那麼多，」艾倫說：「你去了馮·德·萊登家，因為大家都不肯在晚宴上和我見面。你在波福特家的舞會上宣布你們訂婚的消息，這樣就有兩個家族站在我這邊。」

這時候，娜塔莎拿著一封電報進

來，打斷了他們。電報是發給伯爵夫人的，從聖奧古斯丁發來。

西 聯 電 報 公 司

收件人：艾倫・歐蘭斯卡伯爵夫人
來自：聖奧古斯丁的電報

外婆的電報奏效。爸媽同意
復活節後成婚。正發電報給
紐藍。高興到不知說什麼。
好愛你。懷著感謝的梅

P. 62

半個小時之後，當亞契回到家時，他看到一個相似的信封，裡面的訊息也是來自梅。

西 聯 電 報 公 司

收件人：紐藍・亞契
來自：聖奧古斯丁的電報

父母同意婚禮。復活節後的
星期二。十二點。恩典堂。
八位伴娘。請去見牧師。好
幸福。愛你的梅

亞契開始發抖，並查看日誌。他妹妹出來看出了什麼事。

「紐藍！但願電報裡不是壞消息。」

「沒事，除了我要在一個月內結婚。」

他仰起頭，笑了好一會兒。

9. 婚禮

P. 63

這一天涼爽宜人，吹著生氣勃勃的春風，揚起灰塵。紐藍・亞契站在恩典堂的臺階上等著新娘。

婚禮的各項事宜他都打點好了：給伴娘的花束、給伴郎的領針、回禮的謝卡、給主教的紅包。在他準備好要踏上的這條道路上，凡事都很簡單，卻也都令人痛苦。

韓德爾的進行曲響起，新郎環顧教堂。

「這就像歌劇的首演之夜。」他心想，眼前都是同樣的面孔。

他忽然想起自己認為婚禮並不重要，但現在張羅著自己的婚禮，感覺就像是一場人生模仿秀。

P. 65

「真正的人住在某個地方，真正的事件發生在他們身上。」他想。

「紐藍，她來了！」伴郎悄聲說。

亞契睜開眼睛（眼睛真的閉上了嗎？）不一會兒，梅就站在他身邊，然後戒指套上了她的手指，接著他們走出教堂，朝著要載他們去明葛特夫人家參加婚宴的馬車走去。亞契一邊開心地和新娘說著話，一邊感到自己落入黑暗的深淵愈來愈深。

婚宴過後，這對新人前往車站，出發去萊恩貝克，他們要在那裡度過新婚之夜。亞契看著梅：她還是昨天那個單純的女孩，而他感覺卻像個陌生人。

「但願艾倫有來參加婚禮。」她突然說，亞契覺得自己的世界就在四周崩落。

10. 蜜月

P. 66

紐藍·亞契夫婦出發往歐洲度了三個月的蜜月。在巴黎待了一個月，請裁縫師製作衣服後，梅想去游泳和去瑞士爬山，兩人便前往。在抵達倫敦之前，兩人先在諾曼第海邊的一個小地方做了停留。梅對旅行的興致，不如紐藍預期的高。

在這段時間裡，亞契對婚姻失去了熱情。學朋友那樣順著妻子，會容易些。他知道不管發生什麼事，她都會對他忠誠，他也承諾會這樣對她。

婚姻

• 亞契在故事一開始時，對婚姻的看法是什麼？
• 他現在的看法是什麼？
• 什麼改變了？

P. 67

他們在離開倫敦之前，紐藍和梅獲邀和卡佛萊夫人共進晚餐，她是紐藍母親的舊熟識。

「卡佛萊夫人家很可能沒什麼人，」在他們駕車穿越倫敦時，亞契說：「你把自己打扮得太漂亮了！」

「我不想讓他們覺得我們穿得像野

蠻人。」梅嘲笑地回答。

亞契説對了，那是個小型派對，吃過晚餐後，女士們到客廳去，留下亞契和里維耶先生聊天，他是卡佛萊家的法文家教。他們談著書本、文明和知識自由，讓亞契感覺新鮮空氣進入肺部。

「我們聊得很愉快，那個法國年輕人是個有趣的人，我們談論書本和局勢。」他在返家的馬車裡告訴梅。

「那個法國人？他不是很普通嗎？」梅大聲説，「如果他很聰明，我也不會知道。」她補充道。

亞契不喜歡她使用「普通」和「聰明」的字眼，他開始害怕，他很容易注意到她身上他不喜歡的部分。

「啊，那我不會請他來吃晚餐！」他笑著答道。

他很訝異地想到，現在這就是他的未來了。他只能期望，結婚的前半年總是最難熬的，之後生活應該就會變得比較容易。

11. 射箭比賽

P. 68

隨著兩人逐漸適應新生活，紐藍不能説娶了梅是錯誤的決定。她很漂亮，人緣好，是最明理的妻子。他依自己的意思布置自己的新圖書室，又開始和老朋友相聚，在律師事務所上班，也會外出用餐或在家招待朋友。

他們生活愉快，他覺得自己對歐蘭斯卡伯爵夫人的感情只是一時的迷戀，她留在他的記憶中，是一群幽靈中的最後一個。

他站在波福特家的陽台上，想著這一切，這裡正在舉行八月的年度紐波特射箭比賽。梅快要贏得比賽了，這是和槌球一樣受歡迎的運動。射箭被視為一項古典而優雅的運動，比賽這天是紐約各家族的重要社交活動。

紐藍站在那裡觀賞比賽，無意間聽到主人在談梅的獲勝。

「那是她唯一能射中的目標。」波福特説，這讓亞契很生氣。

P. 69

他怕波福特會發現，在梅的善良和沉著的簾幕後面，只是一片空洞。他覺得她從來沒有掀開過那塊簾幕。她很單純，對每個人都很好，沒有人有辦法妒忌她。

梅

- 梅是怎樣的人？
- 你覺得亞契說「掀開簾幕」
  是什麼意思？

　　他們在射箭比賽後駕車回家時，梅突然提議要去看外婆，跟她說自己得了冠軍。

　　明葛特夫人讚賞梅贏得的鑽石箭，捏著梅的手臂說：「你一定要把這個留給你的大女兒。」

　　生小孩這個念頭讓梅臉紅了，最後大家因這樣的難為情而笑成一團。

`P. 70`

　　在他們停留時，得知歐蘭斯卡夫人也在那裡。她這一天從普茲茅斯過來陪明葛特夫人，她住在一戶叫布蘭卡的人家裡。

　　明葛特夫人呼喚艾倫，女僕說她往海邊的小徑走下去了。

　　「跑去帶她回來，紐藍。」明葛特夫人說。

　　亞契站起身來，彷彿在夢中。雖然他是聽說了艾倫在他和梅結婚後的生活，但如今在射箭比賽這一天，她又再度活生生地出現。

彷彿在夢中

- 你覺得這是什麼意思？
- 亞契對艾倫的感覺如何？

12. 在碼頭

`P. 71`

　　亞契走下小徑，看到木製碼頭的盡頭處有座涼亭。一名女子背對著海岸站在那裡，靠著欄杆。那是艾倫。

　　亞契和艾倫都沒有動靜，他站在堤岸邊好一會兒，凝望著大海。她看向大海，看著那些遊艇、帆船和漁船，有一艘帆船正滑行通過萊姆岩燈塔與海岸間的水道。

亞契想：「如果她在帆船通過萊姆岩燈塔之前沒有轉過身來，我就回去。」

她沒有動作。他轉身，走上山坡。

亞契

• 亞契為什麼不和艾倫說話？
• 他感覺如何？

P. 73

亞契不確定他是否想再見到艾倫，但他無法不想她。她在海邊的那個記憶畫面，感覺比他當下的生活更接近他。

他現在有一種強烈的欲望，想看看她住的地方。當席勒頓家為布蘭卡家舉行一場夏末的派對時，他意識到有機會滿足自己的好奇心了。他覺得，如果他可以看到她走過的那塊土地，世界看起來可能就不會那麼空虛。

他打算在派對那天去布蘭卡家，那時不會有人在家。他會說，他有興趣向附近的農場買匹馬。

這一天來臨時，一切都很完美。他到了那裡，站在大門邊，高興地觀賞著那個地方。接著，他朝花園走去。涼亭裡有個色彩鮮亮的東西，看起來像是一把粉紅色的陽傘，這把傘像磁鐵一樣吸引著他，他確定那是艾倫的傘。

他撿起傘，把傘貼近臉頰，聞著味道。他聽到身後有人，等著艾倫的聲音和碰觸，但那是布蘭卡家的女兒！她很友善，但也很驚訝看到亞契在花園裡。

P. 74

她問道：「今天下午，席勒頓家為我們所有人開了一場花園派對，這你不知道嗎？我因為喉嚨痛，就沒有過去。」

當亞契問起歐蘭斯卡夫人是否有去參加時，布蘭卡小姐驚訝地看著他。

「歐蘭斯卡夫人被人叫走了！從波士頓來了封電報，她說她可能要離開兩天。」

「我明天要去波士頓，你知道在哪裡……？」

「當然！她住在帕克旅館。」她繼續談著艾倫。

亞契沒在聽。

13. 波士頓

P. 75

第二天，亞契抵達太陽火辣辣的波士頓，他派人送訊息到歐蘭斯卡夫人住的派克旅館。在未收到回覆之前，他決定去波士頓公園散步，那是位於市中心的一個大公園。他開始穿越公園，此時看到她坐在一棵樹下的第一張長椅上。

他走向她，艾倫轉過身來看著他。

「噢！」她一臉驚訝，然後慢慢露出愉快的微笑。

「我來談公事，才剛到，」亞契解釋說，「你在這裡做什麼？」他繼續說，不太知道自己在說什麼。

「我也是來談公事。」她答道。

「你的髮型不一樣。」他說道，一顆心怦怦跳。

「那是因為娜塔莎沒有和我一起來。我只在這裡待兩天。」她答道。

「你一個人住在派克旅館？」亞契問。

「是的。怎麼了，你覺得那裡很危險嗎？」艾倫答道。

「沒有，不危險，但不符合常規。」

P. 76

「我想也是，我沒有想到這一點。我剛做了更不符合常規的事情，我拒絕拿回屬於我的錢。」她解釋。

「有人帶著提議來找你？」他想知道。

艾倫點點頭。

「你之所以拒絕，是因為所提出的條件嗎？」

「我拒絕了。」

「條件是什麼？」他再問了一次。

「不是什麼難事，只是偶爾坐在他的宴會桌上當女主人。」她解釋。

接著一小段沉默。亞契的心猛然地停了。

「他想要你回去，不計任何代價？」他緊張地問。

「對，用了很大的代價。至少對我來說是很大的代價。」

「所以，你來這裡見他。」亞契做出結論。

「我丈夫？在這裡？」艾倫開始大笑，「他這個季節都在考斯或巴登。他沒來，而是派了別人來。」

「他的祕書？」亞契小心翼翼地問。

「是的。他還在這裡，他堅持要等到今天晚上，以防萬一我改變主意。」她說。然後，她看著他的臉，再度開口：「你都沒變，紐藍。」

他想要回答：「我變了，直到我又見到你。」但他沒有，反而是很快地站起來，看著四周，然後開始說話。

154

P. 77

「和我共度一天！我會説任何你想聽的話，或什麼都不説。除非你要我開口，否則我不會張嘴。我想要的只是和你共度一段時間，我想要的只是聽你説話，我想要帶你遠離那個男人。他什麼時候會到旅館？」

「十一點。」她忐忑不安地回答。

「那我們現在就得離開了，」他説：「我只想要聽到你的消息，知道你都在做什麼。從我們上次見面後，已經過了一百年，也許又要再過一百年才能再度相見。」

此時，她變得很焦慮。

「我在奶奶家那天，你為什麼沒有走下海邊來帶我？」她問道。

「因為你沒有四下環顧，也因為你不知道我在那裡。我下了決定，除非你往四周看，否則我就不去找你。」他笑起來，意識到這有多麼幼稚。

「但我不會故意四處張望。」

「故意？」

「我知道你在那裡。當你駕車進去時，我認出那輛馬車，所以我才走去海邊的。」

「為了盡可能遠離我？」

她低聲重覆道：「為了盡可能遠離你。」

P. 78

在坦白這些心裡的話之後，歐蘭斯卡夫人和紐藍走回旅館，給歐蘭斯卡伯爵的祕書留張便條。艾倫把便條拿進旅館，亞契焦慮地在外面等候。

當他在外面來回踱步時，他看到一個很眼熟的男人消失在人群中，像是個外國人。接著，旅館的大門再度打開，她又來到亞契身邊。

他們坐船觀光，沉默地坐在半空的船裡，享受著他們的親密時光。當他們停下來吃午餐時，艾倫告訴亞契，她厭倦了紐約的社會，決定去華盛頓試試看，看看不同的人，有不同的見識。

「我不明白你為什麼不回歐洲。」亞契聽著她説話，大聲説道。

「我想是因為你。」艾倫答道。

這句告白讓亞契很難為情，不知所措。

「因為我？我會娶某個女人，是因為奉了另一個女人之命。」他回答。

「你答應過今天不提這些事的。」她答道。

「女人就是這個樣子！不想面對不好的事情。」

「對梅來説是不好的事嗎？她會怎麼想？這是我們要思考的事情。」艾倫溫柔地説出表妹的名字。

梅和艾倫

- 艾倫覺得梅是什麼樣的人？
- 梅覺得艾倫是什麼樣的人？

「你讓我看見真實的人生，然後卻要我過虛假的生活。我再也無法忍受了。」亞契說。

「我也無法忍受。」艾倫回答，靜靜地哭了起來。

有好一會兒，他們就這樣親密而安全地待在那裡。他們兩人都知道，他們的命運是分開的。

「你什麼時候要回去？」亞契喊道，但他真正要問的是：「我要如何留住你？」

「我還沒有要回去。」她答道。

「你這是什麼人生啊！」亞契說。

「噢，只要那是你人生的一部分。」艾倫答道。

「我的人生是你的一部分嗎？」亞契回問。

艾倫沒有應聲，只是點頭。然後，他們坐在那裡，只是遠遠地握著彼此的手。

「別不快樂。」她說。

「你不回去？」他回答。

「我不回去。」她說，結束了兩人的對話。

14. 艾倫的未來

在回紐約的路上，亞契感到很平靜，覺得自己好像被金色的光暈環繞住。他離開火車站時，他在派克旅館看到的紳士走向他，和他打招呼。

那是里維耶先生，那個他和梅在倫敦見過的法國人。亞契忽然明白，他就是歐蘭斯卡夫人的丈夫派到波士頓，要說服艾倫回歐洲的祕書。

里維耶向亞契解釋，當他最初來到美國時，他相信伯爵夫人回到丈夫身邊對她最好。他和艾倫的家人談過，他們認同這個想法。亞契了解，他被排除在這些討論之外。

接著，令亞契吃驚的是，里維耶求他不要讓她回去。他們在波士頓見過面後，他知道艾倫變了。她是美國人，對像她這樣的人來說，回到丈夫身邊是不可能的。兩位男士握了握手之後，里維耶先生轉身離開。

P. 82

兩個月過後，在亞契夫人的十一月例行感恩節晚餐上，紐藍清楚看出歐蘭斯卡夫人的家人不再資助她。就算是曼森·明葛特夫人，也無法為她決定不回到丈夫身邊的決定做辯護。

就像梅的媽媽所說的，大家只是「讓可憐的艾倫自己找生路」。他們說她成了「波西米亞人」。紐藍注意到，當艾倫的名字被提起時，梅臉紅了，她也不支持表姐艾倫。似乎所有人都改變了對她的看法。

從他們共度的那個炎熱夏日之後，亞契和歐蘭斯卡夫人就沒說過話。他知道她回華盛頓了，和她母親住在一起。

他捎信給她，問他們何時能再碰面，她回了兩個字：「還沒」。

晚餐時，人們談起朱利亞斯·波福特的生意問題，他們擔心大家在經濟上都會遭受波及。

席勒頓·傑克森說，很可惜，歐蘭斯卡夫人拒絕接受丈夫的提議。

他說：「簡而言之，她現在要靠什麼維生？」

「現在？」亞契問道。

P. 83

「我從她奶奶那裡得知，家族因為她拒絕這個提議而縮減了她的津貼。她大部分的錢都和波福特一起投資，現在那些投資也可能也沒了。」

「我確定她現在不會回去了。」亞契答道。

「那是你的看法，她得想辦法活下去。歐蘭斯卡夫人也許能說服她奶奶給她錢，但我們知道她的家族不想把她留在美國這裡。」

當梅和亞契在感恩節晚餐後回到家時，亞契宣布，他近期因工作的關係，要前往華盛頓。梅知道他為什麼突然對去華盛頓有興趣，但她沒有跟亞契說，她只是建議他應該去看艾倫。亞契知道，妻子很清楚他想去華盛頓的真正原因。

15. 明葛特夫人中風

P. 84

接下來的那個星期三,亞契去上班時,雷特布雷先生一臉憂心地去找他。波福特完蛋了,而且他把很多人一起拖下水,這是華爾街史上最大的金融災難。在他們談話時,亞契收到一封梅的信。

明葛特老夫人前一天晚上中風,梅的家人需要亞契過去。他立刻動身。梅在門口等他,臉色蒼白但掛著微笑。他得知蕾吉娜·波福特前一晚曾來拜訪明葛特老夫人,請求資助自己的丈夫。

「當他讓你戴滿珠寶時,你的名字是波福特,當他現在讓你帶滿羞恥時,你還是要叫作波福特。」明葛特夫人對蕾吉娜說。

波福特夫人在一小時後離開,明葛特夫人隨後上床,看得出來心煩意亂。清晨三點,她按鈴求救。

包括亞契在內,全家人都同意妻子的家是在丈夫那裡,而妻子和丈夫的連結,要比妻子和妻子的家族更強。

P. 86

幸好中風並不嚴重,明葛特夫人很快又能再次下達命令。她要女僕發

電報給艾倫·歐蘭斯卡,要她來看奶奶。亞契發了電報,並主動提議去澤西火車站接艾倫。

梅聽到紐藍再也不必去華盛頓時很意外。他知道妻子清楚自己撒了謊,妻子卻佯裝不知,這讓他覺得很不好受。

當他動身時,他只想到從澤西到明葛特夫人家的途中,他有兩個小時可以和艾倫共處。

亞契在一個下雪的暗沉下午,在澤西市車站踱步等待艾倫。他想像她下火車時,自己遠遠地就看到她。他要告訴她好多事情,多到難以置信。

等待

- 亞契在等艾倫的火車來時，感覺如何？請打勾：
  - ☐ 緊張　☐ 興奮　☐ 快樂
  - ☐ 苦惱　☐ 困惑
- 你曾經在等候某個人時有過這樣的感覺嗎？

P. 87

「這邊，我有馬車。」他説，一邊用手拉著她的手臂。

「奶奶好嗎？」艾倫輕聲問道。

「她好多了，沒事，真的。」亞契説，握著艾倫的手。

然後他脱下她緊貼的棕色手套，親吻她的手心。

「你沒想到我今天會來嗎？」他問道。

「噢，沒有。」她答道。

「我幾乎不記得你了，但你知道，總是像這樣，每次你都重新再和我相遇。」亞契説。

「噢，是的，我知道，我知道！」艾倫答道，坦承有相同的感覺。

他們坐在一起，討論著里維耶先生的拜訪，以及他如何幫助艾倫擺脱丈夫。艾倫的坦率讓亞契很驚訝，她覺得生命中的這些事件讓她變得更堅強。

「我的淚水已乾。」她對亞契説。

「你要知道，我們之間不能再這樣繼續下去了。」亞契對她説。

「為什麼不能？」艾倫想知道。

「我們在一起，又不在一起。」

「你今天不該來這裡。」艾倫説，然後忽然親吻了他。

P. 88

「你遠超過我記憶中的樣子，我想要的不只是偶爾和你共度一、兩個小時而已。我可以在你身邊耐心等待著，暗自相信這會實現。」亞契説。

「你覺得我應該和你一起，即使我不能成為你的妻子？」艾倫問他。

「我想要設法和你逃走，去一個我們可以單純相愛的世界，成為彼此生命的全部。」

「噢，親愛的，那個地方在哪裡？」艾倫嘆了一口氣，取笑他。

「那你對我們兩個人有什麼計畫？」他問道。

「我們？沒有我們，我們沒有未來。」艾倫答道。

亞契靜靜坐著，一陣尖鋭的痛楚令他暈眩。接著，他停下馬車，留下艾倫獨自一人，説道：「你説得對，我今天不應該來的。」

他哭了起來，感覺眼淚凍結在睫毛上。

16. 在紐約獨處

P. 89

那天晚上，紐藍和梅坐在家中的圖書室裡。亞契在看一本歷史書，梅在刺繡，亞契突然意識到他們極度單調的生活，梅決不會出現無法預期的情緒或想法來讓他吃驚。他放下書本，焦躁地站起來。

「怎麼了？」

「這裡好熱，我需要一點空氣。」他打開窗戶，把上半身探出到黑暗而冰冷的冬夜裡。

「紐藍，關上窗戶，你會生病。」梅對著他大喊。

之後他心裡想著：「我已經死了好幾個月、好幾個月了。」

有一天，曼森‧明葛特夫人要求見他，他希望會有機會見到艾倫。當他來到明葛特夫人家，得知艾倫出門了，明葛特老夫人想要單獨和他談話。

P. 90

「好了，已經決定了！艾倫要和我住，不管家族怎麼説！」她立刻説。

亞契沉默地聽著。他以前想過，他們可能可以旅居很遠的地方，過著幸福的日子，也許可以去日本。他很震驚地離開，朝波福特家走去，希望在那裡找到艾倫。

「艾倫，我現在可以見到你了，我們會在一起。」當他看到她在街上時，他唐突地説道。

「啊，奶奶告訴你了？」她答道。

「我明天一定要見你，找個我們可以獨處的地方。」亞契説。

「在紐約獨處？」艾倫問道。

「公園裡的藝術博物館，兩點半和我在那裡見面，我會在門口。」

她轉過身，快步走進馬車，他覺得她揮了揮手。

「她會來的！」他對自己説。

「我想，你會來紐約，是因為你害怕。」第二天在博物館裡，亞契對她説。

「害怕？」艾倫問道。

「怕我去華盛頓看你。」

「嗯，是的。」她説。

「所以呢？」他問道。

「嗯，所以這樣比較好，不是嗎？」她嘆氣。

P. 91

「不，我跟你説過我想要的是什麼。」亞契説。

「我答應過要和奶奶住，因為我覺得我在那裡會比較安全。」

「遠離我？這比愛我更安全？」亞契問道。

「我不能和她住，然後欺瞞家人。」艾倫答道。

「所以我才要你和我一起走！」亞契說。

「我得走了。」艾倫說。

「我們明天再碰個面吧。」亞契請求她。

「後天。」她好一會兒後答道。

「親愛的！」他說。

「噢，我要遲到了，再見。」

她匆忙離開，等她走到門口時，她轉過身一會兒，對他揮了揮手。

等亞契回到家，他很驚訝地發現梅還沒回來。他走進圖書室，坐在扶手椅上。

當大門打開，梅走進來時，他還無聲地坐在那裡。

「我回來得太晚了，你不是在擔心我吧，有嗎？」她問道。

亞契看起來很困惑，「很晚了嗎？」

P. 92

「七點多了。我去看外婆，艾倫散步回來時我正要離開，所以我就留了下來，和她聊了好久。我們已經有好久沒有這樣好好說過話了。她好善良，就像以前的艾倫。我很擔心自己近來沒有善待她。她和其他人不一樣，但我不想批評她。」

亞契意識到梅其實有多恨艾倫，而她又是多麼努力要處理這種情緒。

情感

- 梅感覺如何？
- 亞契感覺如何？
- 他們對彼此誠實嗎？
- 為什麼？為什麼沒有？

17. 歡送晚宴

P. 93

馮‧德‧萊登家返回紐約，以支援被波福特危機所波及的家族。

這天晚上，他們邀請梅和紐藍一起去聽歌劇。梅穿著新娘禮服，因為在習俗上，新娘在新婚後的一、兩年要穿上結婚禮服。所以就像兩年前的那個夜晚，梅穿著白色禮服，而舞台上的是浮士德。他們聆賞著音樂，亞契突然離場，並要梅和他一起走。

等他們回到家，亞契覺得有必要和梅表白自己的感覺。

「歐蘭斯卡夫人……」他開口，但梅打斷了他。

「現在都無所謂了，一切都結束了。」她說。

161

亞契一臉茫然地看著她，「都結束了，這是什麼意思？」

「她很快就要回歐洲了，奶奶接受了她的決定，並給她足夠的錢，讓她可以獨立生活。」

亞契很難控制住自己。

P. 94

「不可能，」他大叫：「你是怎麼知道這件事的？」

「我昨天見到艾倫，我告訴過你，我在外婆家見到她。」

「她昨天告訴你的？」

「不是，我今天下午收到她的便條。」

然後，她走向亞契，把他冰冷的手放在她的臉頰上。

梅提議辦一場大晚宴，由這對年輕夫妻第一次做東道主，來和艾倫告別，連馮·德·萊登夫婦也為了這次活動而留在紐約。

一切都張羅得很完美：菜單卡、燈具、餐桌、花飾、銀籃和蠟燭。家族裡最重要的成員和友人都獲邀，艾倫享受著整場宴會上大家對她的關注。

亞契坐在艾倫旁邊。他突然意識到，全家人已經注意他好長一段時間，覺得他和艾倫在相戀。他感到自己像是站立在軍營中間的囚犯。

他轉頭跟艾倫聊起美國和歐洲的火車之旅，接著餐桌上的人討論起去義大利旅遊，並同意印度很有意思，應該去看看。

P. 96

注視

• 誰在注視亞契？
• 他們在想什麼？

亞契在家中的玄關最後一次看著艾倫，她要離開了。他想陪她走到馬車，但馮·德·萊登先生說他們會送她回家。

「再見。」艾倫說。

「再見，我很快會在巴黎見到你。」他答道。

「噢，如果你和梅能來……」她說。

他再一次看著她的臉，然後她便離去了。

稍晚在圖書室裡，梅想和紐藍討論晚上的事。

「很美好。我可以進來討論嗎？」她問道。

「當然，但你不是想睡了嗎？」亞契答道。

「不，我不睏，我想和你坐一下。」

「好吧。」他答道。

「前幾天晚上，我原本要告訴你一件事，」亞契繼續說：「我好累，想要去渡假。」

「噢，我看得出來，紐藍！你最近工作太多了！」梅擔心地說。

P. 98

「我想要去長途旅行，遠離一切，」他說：「也許去印度。」

「那麼遠？但恐怕無法成行，親愛的，我的醫生不會讓我和你一起去。紐藍，今天早上，我確定了一件我一直盼望的事情，我懷孕了。」

「噢，親愛的。」他說，把她抱進懷裡。

他們都沒講話。

「你沒有猜到？」梅問道。

「你告訴別人了嗎？」亞契問道。

「只有我媽，還有艾倫。你知道，我告訴過你，我和艾倫有一天下午聊了很久。」

「啊！」亞契大叫，他的心跳停了。

「紐藍，我先告訴了她，你介意嗎？」梅問道。

「怎麼會？」他答道，想保持平靜，「但那是兩個星期以前的事，我以為你是說你到今天早上才確定？」

她臉紅了，看著他，「不，我那時候還不確定，但我告訴艾倫，我懷孕了。你看，我說對了！」她答道，藍色的雙眼閃爍著勝利。

18. 在巴黎

P. 99

紐藍・亞契坐房間裡，他人生大部分的真實事件都是在這裡發生的。在這個房間裡，他的第一個孩子達拉斯受洗；第二個孩子瑪莉宣布和一個無趣但可靠的男子訂婚，還有，他和梅聊著兒子達拉斯和比爾的學業。

紐藍一直是個好公民，是一位受尊敬的律師，大眾看重他的意見。他也是個慈愛的父親、忠實的丈夫。

當梅因肺炎過世時，他真心哀悼她。他所擁有的第一張梅的照片，還放在他的寫字桌上。她終其一生都缺乏想像力，也不會注意到改變，這讓孩子和亞契不會對她透露自己的看法。她過世的時候，覺得這個世界是個美好地方，充滿了甜蜜的家庭，就像她自己的家庭一樣。

亞契坐在那裡想事情時，電話響了。兒子達拉斯從芝加哥打來告訴他，有個客戶要他去義大利看一些花園。他邀請父親在他和芬妮・波福特結婚之前，最後一次以父子的身分去旅行，她是朱利亞斯・波福特第二次結婚所生的漂亮女兒。

P. 100

巴黎讓亞契心中溢滿了年輕時代的混亂和快樂。他從年輕時就沒再來過巴黎，他知道可能會遇到歐蘭斯卡夫人。亞契覺得自己擁有了一切，除了生命之花。

當他想到艾倫，他就把她想成一本他喜愛的書裡的虛構人物。她象徵著他所錯失的一切，而現在他有機會和她重逢。

P. 101

「我有個消息要告訴你，歐蘭斯卡伯爵夫人會在五點半時，等我們兩個

164

過去。」達拉斯在他們抵達巴黎之後
的隔天告訴他父親。

亞契看著他。

「芬妮要我答應她在巴黎要為她做
三件事：幫她找到德布西最後一批歌
曲的總譜，去巴黎大木偶劇場，還有
去看歐蘭斯卡夫人。你知道，她對芬
妮很好，她也是我們的表親。」

亞契繼續盯著兒子，「你跟她說了
我在這裡？」

「當然，為什麼不？她聽起來很和
藹，她是什麼樣的人？」達拉斯答
道。

「和藹？我不知道。她很不一樣。」

「嗯，她是那種讓你想要拋棄一切
的女人嗎？但你沒有。」

「我沒有。」亞契肅穆地說。

「母親在去世的前一天說，我們和
你在一起很安全，因為她有一次要求
你，而你放棄了最想要的東西。」

亞契沉默地看著兒子，之後低聲
地說：「她沒要求過我。」

「不，我忘了，你們沒要求過彼此
任何事。你們彼此什麼事情都不談，
你們只是坐著，看著彼此，猜想暗地
裡發生什麼事。」他兒子答道。

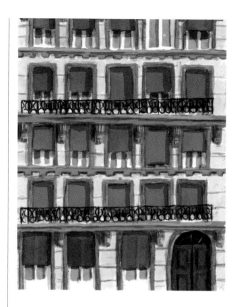

P. 103

下午，達拉斯去凡爾賽，亞契則
去羅浮宮，艾倫跟他說過自己常去那
裡。

父子回到旅館碰面，然後一起走
向艾倫家。他忽然竊竊地自言自言：
「可是我才五十七歲。」

他知道要開始一段新的夏日熱戀
已經來不及了，但當然，一段寧靜的
秋日友誼則不晚。他們之間分隔超過
三十年了，最後一次見面之後，對她
的生活就幾乎一無所知。

亞契和達拉斯抵達艾倫家時，太
陽柔和地閃耀著。那是一棟現代建
築，奶油色的正面有很多窗戶和陽

165

臺。其中一扇窗戶的遮雨蓬還沒拉下來，好讓傍晚最後一線的夕陽照進去。

「門房說在四樓。」達拉斯跟他父親說。

他們兩個都抬頭看著沒有遮雨蓬的那扇窗戶。

「一定是那間了。」達拉斯說。

這時，亞契看到有棵樹下有張空的長椅。

「我要在那裡坐一會。」他告訴達拉斯。

「怎麼了，你不舒服嗎？」達拉斯問道。

「噢，我好得很，但是你自己上去就好。」

「你的意思是你不上來，爸？」

P. 104

「我不知道。」亞契慢慢地說。

「她不會懂的。」達拉斯答道。

「去吧，兒子，也許我會在你後面上去。」

「那我要怎麼跟她說？」達拉斯問道。

「你總是知道要說什麼。」亞契帶著微笑說。

「我會跟她說你是老派人，喜歡走樓梯，不愛搭電梯。」

「說我老派就好。」亞契答道。

亞契坐下來，繼續看著公寓的那扇窗戶。他想像達拉斯走進房間，笑了笑。他想像艾倫站起來，伸出一隻細長的手，上面戴著三隻戒指。

「在這裡，比上樓還要真實。」他突然對自己說。

他在長椅上坐了許久，眼睛盯著陽台看。窗戶透出一道燈光，一名僕人拉上了窗簾。紐藍心想，那就是他一直在等候的信號。他慢慢站起來，獨自走回旅館。

自由之地？

P. 118–119

美國獨立戰爭後，於 1787 年起草美國憲法，第一修正案明確定義了多項的公民自由，以保護公民的權利與自由。

> 美國憲法第一修正案所定義的公民自由包括言論自由、新聞自由、宗教自由、集會自由與請願自由，憲法還增加了哪些自由與權利？

然而，差不多過了一百年後，在《純真年代》的紐約，社會規範與期待深深影響著男女的個人自由。在小說中，透過許多在不同情境下的狀況，提出了自由的問題。

例如，艾倫‧歐蘭斯卡不能乾脆和丈夫離婚，然後自己住在自己所選擇的紐約地區。家族和其他具有影響力家族的意見，比她自己的願望還重要。她在財務上依靠著家族，而且她無法像周遭的男人那樣去工作來養活自己。

雖然，紐藍‧亞契是個有權勢的人，出身於受人尊敬的家族，但是他的個人自由也受限。外界期待他娶一個家族認可的對象，不管他是否愛她。

這些角色的個人自由，在日常生活上或多或少也受到限制，要去哪裡、該何時外出、要穿什麼樣的衣服、要和誰交談，都有不成文的常規，人們應該要遵守。女性的選擇權尤其更加受限。

今天的個人自由

P. 120–121

　　從十九世紀之後產生了很多的變遷，而各個社會階級、文化背景或國家的改變與發展，變遷的速度都不一樣。在大部分國家，個人的自由都受到法律保障，但是並不是每個人都感受到自己擁有所必需的公民自由，能讓自己成為自由的個體。有時候這是由於宗教衝突，有些則是政治決策的關係。

　　網路時代讓「個人自由」這個老問題顯現在新的情境下。言論自由、隱私問題和資料保護是現在的熱門議題，社群媒體的傳播帶來個人自由的新問題。你如何確知你的身分受到保護？言論自由如何受到社群媒體的影響？

　　從不同的觀點來看，個人自由也是個人的、心理的問題。我們真的能擺脫他人的期待和我們自己社會的規範嗎？個人自由對你的意義是什麼？

英國大憲章（1215）

大憲章（Magna Carta）取自中世紀的拉丁文，是英國第一部定義公民權和自由的法律文件。

今日，大憲章中的大部分條文都已重新修定或廢除，但有些最初的原則仍保留在全世界的重要憲政文件中，包括美國的權利法案（1791）、英國1689年的權利法案（1689）、聯合國的世界人權宣言（1948）和歐洲的人權公約（1950）。

Answer Key

Before Reading

Pages 18–19

1 Newland Archer agrees with the conventions of his friends.

2 a T b T c T d F

4 a late b drawing room
c mysterious d simple
e voice

Pages 20–21

6 a 2 b 3 c 4 d 1

7 a moral values
b member
c gossip
d scandal
e labyrinth
f pyramid

8
• **MALE**: Mr, Monsieur, Count, Duke
• **FEMALE**: Mrs, Miss, Madame, Countess

9 a 6 b 1 c 4 d 2
e 5 f 3

10 a engagement
b marriage
c wedding
d honeymoon

Page 25

ELLEN OLENSKA

• She had just left her husband and had run away with her husband secretary. She had lived alone in Venice. Her husband was a brute.

Page 39

FUNNY HOUSE

1. She wants to feel loved and safe.
2. Fashion is important to her family.

Page 56

NOTE

• "Come late tomorrow: I must explain to you. Ellen."

Page 57

FLOWERS

• Newland Archer—May,
(lilies-of-the-valley, every morning)
• Newland Archer—Ellen
(yellow roses, twice)
• Mr Beaufort—Ellen
• Mr van der Luyden—Ellen
• Count Olenski—Ellen
• Ellen—one of her neighbors

Page 66

MARRIAGE

• He seemed to be looking forward to marriage with May. Now he has no enthusiasm for marriage.

Page 96

WATCHING

• The whole family—including: Mrs Welland, Mrs Archer and the van der Luydens.
• They are thinking Ellen and Newland are lovers.

AFTER READING

Page 106

TALK ABOUT THE STORY
2 [a] Ellen

Pages 107

COMPREHENSION
1 [a] F [b] T [c] F [d] F
[e] T [f] F [g] F [h] F

2
[a] Newland Archer wanted to arrive late to the opera.
[c] Countess Olenska had an unhappy marriage.
[d] Mr Beaufort was not a respected man.
[f] May and Newland didn't enjoy their long European honeymoon.
[g] May and Newland had three children.
[h] Newland decided not to meet Ellen in Paris.

3 possible answers:
[a] At the opera.
[b] Archer was afraid that the Mingotts would bring the Countess Olenska to the ball.
[c] They are cousins.
[d] Countess Olenska had left her husband and run away to live alone in Venice.
[e] Mrs Manson Mingott.
[f] The Beauforts have a luxurious lifestyle but "shameful" past. Mrs Beaufort comes from an old but poor family in the South.

Mr Beaufort is a hospitable Englishman, but he has secrets. He is not respected.

Pages 108–109

4 [a] 2 [b] 3 [c] 1
5 possible answers:
[a] Ellen and Archer kiss for the first time in Ellen's "funny little house" in New York. Archer has just told her he loves her.
[b] Ellen and Archer go on a boat trip together in Boston. They talk about their relationship and their future. Ellen cries.
[c] Ellen enters the drawing room at the van der Luydens' house, for an important dinner. Archer notices her mysterious beauty and simple behavior. She is not as stylish as everyone has expected her to be.

CHARACTERS
1 [a] superior [b] different
[c] reasonable [d] dared
[e] secrets [f] shy
[g] aristocracy
[h] interesting

Pages 110–111

3
• **Ellen Olenska**: likes art, different, yellow roses, mysterious, black sheep of the family
• **May Welland**: sporty, conventional, lilies-of-the-valley, innocent, popular

171

4
  [a] Mr van der Luyden
  [b] Newland Archer
  [c] Ellen Olenska
  [d] Mrs Mingott

5
[a] Mrs Archer at the van der Luydens'.
[b] Ellen at Jersey City Station.
[c] Archer at Ellen's house.
[d] Mrs Welland at Mrs Mingott's house.

VOCABULARY

2 [a] gazing   [b] reddened
   [c] nodded   [d] trembling
   [e] glanced   [f] stare
   [g] sighed

3 [a] 2   [b] 1   [c] 4
   [d] 3   [e] 5   [f] 6

Pages 112–113

4 [a] admired   [b] despises
   [c] consent   [d] adored
   [e] persuaded   [f] pretend

5 [a] 6   [b] 1   [c] 3
   [d] 2   [e] 4   [f] 5

LANGUAGE

1 [a] 3   The Beauforts
   [b] 4   The Beauforts
   [c] 1   Ellen
   [d] 5   Ellen
   [e] 2   Ellen

2 possible answers:
   [a] escape with somebody
   [b] similar in appearance or character to an older member of the same family

[c] stop trying to do something
[d] escape
[e] begin a journey
[f] finally be in a particular situation

3 [a] ran away with
   [b] takes after
   [c] to give up
   [d] to get away
   [e] set off
   [f] ended up

Pages 114–115

4 possible answers:
• The word "missus" tells us Beaufort has more common origins than the others in New York high society. It is an informal word and one unlikely to be used by the upper classes. We learn he spends time with the "bohemians" of society, who are perhaps not considered suitable company by the others in high class society.

5 possible answers:
[a] "It is a bad sign that you are impatient."
[b] May asked Newland if anything had happened.
[c] "The Countess Olenska lived alone in Venice."
[d] She said her dress wasn't smart enough.

PLOT AND THEME

1 [a] 6   [b] 2   [c] 1   [d] 4
   [e] 5   [f] 3   [g] 8   [h] 7

2 Various answers, but the basic events are:

[a] Archer sees Ellen for the first time.

[b] May and Archer announce their engagement.

[c] Ellen writes to Archer from the van der Luydens'. Archer follows her there and they talk. Julius Beaufort arrives, and Archer leaves.

[d] Ellen meets with her husband's secretary. Archer and Ellen spend a day together.

[e] May and Archer go on their honeymoon. They visit dressmakers in Paris. Then they go swimming and mountaineering in Switzerland. Finally, they dine with Mrs Carfry in London.

[f] Ellen avoids Archer by going to the pier. Archer watches Ellen but doesn't talk to her.

[g] Archer goes to visit May to convince her of a short engagement.

[h] Over 30 years later, Archer and his son go to visit Ellen's apartment, but Archer doesn't go into the building.

Pages 116–117

3 possible answers:
- Pyramid is the structure of importance of families in New York society based on family, wealth and class.
- Labyrinth is the rules of the New York high society to an outsider.

5 possible answers:
- She left her husband, ran away with her husband's secretary, and lived alone in Venice.
- She wants a divorce, is not stylish, likes living in a part of New York that isn't "fashionable", cries in public, tells the truth about how she feels, and walks or stays in places without a man to accompany her.

EXAM

Pages 122–123

1 1) b 2) c 3) d
4) a 5) a 6) b

2
[a] 1) like 2) them 3) who
4) were
[b] 1) where 2) that 3) from
4) order 5) with

TEST

Pages 124–125

1 [a] 1 [b] 2 [c] 1 [d] 1
2 [a] 4 [b] 2 [c] 1 [d] 4
[e] 3 [f] 3 [g] 2 [h] 2

Helbling Classics 寂天經典文學讀本

Helbling Fiction 寂天現代文學讀本

國家圖書館出版品預行編目資料

純真年代 / Edith Wharton 著；Nora Nagy
改寫；蔡裴驊 譯. 一初版. 一[臺北市]：寂天
文化, 2019.10 面；公分. 中英對照；
譯自：The Age of Innocence

ISBN 978-986-318-831-5 (平裝附光碟片)
　　　1. 英語　　2. 讀本

805.18　　　　　　　　　　108012622

純真年代

原著 _ Edith Wharton

改寫 _ Nora Nagy

插畫 _ Simone Manfrini

譯者 _ 蔡裴驊

校對 _ 陳慧莉

編輯 _ 安卡斯

製程管理 _ 洪巧玲

出版者 _ 寂天文化事業股份有限公司

電話 _ +886-2-2365-9739

傳真 _ +886-2-2365-9835

網址 _ www.icosmos.com.tw

讀者服務 _ onlineservice@icosmos.com.tw

出版日期 _ 2019年10月 初版一刷（250101）

郵撥帳號 _ 1998620-0 寂天文化事業股份有限公司